"I've been waiting quite a while for this moment..."

István shut the door. "You and I are going to enjoy ourselves, Tanya. Just the two of us."

"I don't know what you mean," she grated.

"Don't you?"

The sexual implication, the invitation, was plain enough. She whisked her damp palms down her hips, immobilized by her leaden body. And she knew then that he couldn't be her brother.

DESTINY awaits us all, and for Tanya, Mariann and Suzanne Evans—all roads lead east to the mysteries of Hungary.

Tangled Destinies
As Tanya arrives in Hungary for her younger brother's wedding, her older brother, István, lies in wait after four years. He's the only man she's ever loved—and he's hurt her. But what he has to tell her will change the course of her life forever.

Unchained Destinies
Editor Mariann Evans is on a publishing mission in Budapest. But instead of duping rival publisher Vigadó Gábor, she is destined to fall into his arms.

Threads of Destiny
Suzanne Evans' attendance at the double wedding of her sister Tanya and her brother, John, presents a fateful meeting with mysterious gate-crasher Lásló Huszár. He's the true heir to a family fortune and he has a young family of his own. He is about to make sure that his complex family history is inextricably linked with hers, as all the elements of this compelling trilogy are woven together.

A Note to the Reader:

This novel is the first part of a trilogy. Each novel is independent and can be read on its own. It is the author's suggestion, however, that they be read in the order written.

SARA WOOD

Tangled Destinies

DESTINY
BOOK
1

Harlequin Books

TORONTO • NEW YORK • LONDON
AMSTERDAM • PARIS • SYDNEY • HAMBURG
STOCKHOLM • ATHENS • TOKYO • MILAN
MADRID • WARSAW • BUDAPEST • AUCKLAND

ISBN 0-373-11790-6

TANGLED DESTINIES

First North American Publication 1996.

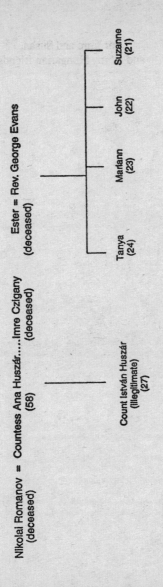

Nikolai Romanov = Countess Ana Huszár.....Imre Czigany
(deceased)   (58)   (deceased)

Ester = Rev. George Evans
(deceased)

Tanya   Mariann   John   Suzanne
(24)   (23)   (22)   (21)

Count István Huszár
(Illegitimate)
(27)

For Imre and Susan,
and all my Hungarian friends

CHAPTER ONE

'YOU'RE obsessed with István,' said Mariann airily. 'Of *course* he won't be there! *Him*, go to a *wedding*?'

Tanya bent her chestnut head and moved pensively behind the queue that wound backwards and forwards like a slow-moving snake digesting a rat and István was brought even more intensely to mind. Snake, rat...

'He might,' she frowned. 'He had a special...soft spot for Lisa.' Her lips pressed together, holding back the information from her sister that it had been more serious than that: a fling of momentous passion with terrible consequences that had split her family apart.

'He never had a soft spot *anywhere*,' scoffed Mariann.

'Heart and mind of stone,' Tanya agreed and tried to make a joke of her fears. 'Well, if he does turn up, I suppose I could rearrange that poker-face of his into something more human!'

'You?' laughed Mariann. 'You wouldn't hurt a fly!'

Tanya smiled thinly, the harder green of her hazel eyes deepening till their melting brown warmth had totally disappeared. No, she wouldn't normally harm a living creature, but she'd make an exception for István and gladly squash him flat!

'I refuse to think of him any more,' she said decisively, and let a smile win through. 'Not when there's a fairy-tale wedding in the offing!' She beamed. Her brother John, her best friend Lisa. What could be nicer? 'Fancy them having the reception in a Hungarian castle! Nothing could be more romantic!'

'Or expensive,' said Mariann drily. 'Unless he gets a discount because he works there. Well, since John's so flush with money from his new job, he'd better pay back

5

what he owes you.' She gave her gentle sister a stern look. 'You're too quick to help us all.'

'That's what you do for family,' smiled Tanya.

'István is "family". That means...you'd welcome him back if he appears?' teased Mariann with a wicked grin.

'No! He's different,' answered Tanya firmly. 'He walked out on us—treated Mum like dirt. I can't forgive him.'

Her sister's eyes twinkled. 'I wonder. He was your idol and you were his devoted slave once.'

'I was a child, fooled by his daring. I didn't know what he was really like,' Tanya replied stiffly.

'Did anyone? All those weeping maidens at our door only saw the brooding Heathcliff figure, galloping across the moors. None of them knew how difficult he was at home.'

'Why are we talking about him again?' complained Tanya.

'You always do,' answered Mariann gently.

She flushed. 'Nonsense! He doesn't exist as far as I'm concerned.' But, she thought, it was sad that their family wasn't complete. If only...

'OK. Focus on the fairy-tale, hon. Give my love to baby brother John and his bride-to-be and start swigging the bubbly without me. You deserve some fun for a change.'

'A week's holiday!' gloated Tanya. It seemed like an eternity. 'After John's wedding I'm going to spend it sitting in cafés eating pastries and——'

'Simpering at handsome gypsy violinists!'

'No, charming John's boss,' corrected Tanya. 'I have to take a break from the violins and sticky buns and get that riding school business! But I mean to make the most of the trip and explore Hungary too. Oh...the queue's moving again. Bye. See you at the castle later on.'

Mariann leaned over the barrier and kissed Tanya affectionately. Two sisters, so different in temperament, so similar in repose with their distinctive high Hungarian cheekbones and mass of dark chestnut hair.

'Oh, boy, do these Hungarians know what's coming? Wait till I've picked up Sue and they've got *three* Evans sisters to contend with!' Mariann did a wiggle that caused a few male eyes to pop. 'There'll be you, tearing at their heartstrings with your dreamy looks——'

'Hardly, with you and Sue around!' laughed Tanya. 'Just cast me as the Ugly Sister——'

Mariann's squawk brought a score of eyes to rest on the blushing Tanya. '*You*? Take a good look in the mirror, hon, and see who's "the fairest of them all",' she said fondly. 'When Sue and I turn up, I expect some handsome Hungarian will have whisked you off on his white horse! Bye. Have a good trip!'

Tanya's earlier sense of foreboding receded in the wake of her sister's daunting cheerfulness. Sticking to her promise to herself, she firmly put aside her worries. István and Lisa's old love-affair *must* be dead and buried, she reasoned, or Lisa wouldn't have agreed to marry John. And so she turned her thoughts to the wedding, pushing back the nagging feeling that István might appear and ruin everyone's happiness again.

When the plane approached the outskirts of Budapest it flew low over towering concrete apartment blocks—relics, perhaps, of the old Communist regime. Their forbidding exteriors made her think of István and how cold, ruthless and unbending he could be. Her brow furrowed. Mariann was right—she was obsessed with his memory.

Her hands became clammy. Maybe she was right to be apprehensive. After all, István *had* gone to Hungary when he'd vanished four years ago. He *could* have seen some announcement about the wedding. And he'd been forced to leave Lisa...

With her stomach churning, she walked gracefully through Customs, concealing only what was going on in her head: István; was he here? Two pink stains flushed her prominent, Slavonic cheekbones and her pace became brisker, almost as though the prospect of seeing him was filling her with a hot energy. People were lined up at the barrier, waving, crying, laughing... but not István.

'Thank heavens!' she muttered, then frowned at the swamping sense of loss that followed the realisation. No dark, cynical eyes on her. No hard, male mouth curled in brotherly contempt. No figure so compelling and yet completely self-contained that he made her feel nervous and awkward in comparison.

'Tanya!' came a familiar yell of delight.

'John! John!' she cried in relief. 'Wonderful to see you!' She embraced her fair-haired brother and her heartbeat returned to near-normal instead of galloping like a frightened colt.

'Dear Tan! Welcome to Hungary! Have we got a *party* this afternoon!' John enthused.

Tanya's sweet smile brought a radiant sheen to her face. 'A party! What fun!'

'How's Dad?' asked John, taking charge of her luggage.

'Much better in himself, though his arthritis is worse. He sends his love and his blessing,' she answered softly.

'Are you sure you can cope?'

'Of course!' she reassured him. Their father had been like a lost soul when their mother had died four years ago. It was as though the light had gone out of his life too and Tanya both envied and feared a love like that.

Taking early retirement on health grounds, he'd turned to her for comfort and companionship—perhaps, she was aware, as a substitute in some way for her mother. Tanya's face grew tender. All her life she'd longed to make a stronger bond with her father and it was some comfort to her too, because her own grief was too much to bear. She needed someone to care for, a purpose in life beyond simply existing. Her mother's death had occurred only three months after István had vanished and the double blow had numbed her completely.

At a family conference, she had quietly convinced her sisters that it made sense for them to continue their careers in London since she was able to work happily

from home. It was she who'd persuaded John to follow
Lisa to Budapest and given him financial help, explaining
to her father that he'd be cruel to stand in his adored
son's way.

John gave her hand a squeeze. 'I'll give Dad a ring
later. Skates on, Tan, no time to waste; it's a fair drive...
Something wrong?' he asked, when she hesitated.

'I—I half wondered——' No István. She *had* expected
him there. Something fluttered in her stomach. Disappointment, definitely. That was strange. 'It's daft, but
I had this *ghastly* idea that István would pop up like
Dracula from his grave and hover about, grinding his
teeth!' She giggled, seeing how silly that was.

John's homely face went pale. 'Let him try,' he
muttered grimly. 'I'd take a sledge-hammer to his head
and ram him back into the hole he crawled from!
Bastard!'

'John! He is our brother,' she remonstrated gently,
hurrying along beside him. John hated István. If he ever
knew what István had actually done to Lisa, she dreaded
to think what might happen.

'Brother? I wonder,' growled John. 'It's only because
Dad's a vicar and Mum was as decent as the day is long
that I've never felt suspicious about his parentage.'

Tanya nodded soberly. She also had felt that István
was different—as though he'd come from another background altogether. He bore absolutely no resemblance
to anyone in their family. 'Bit of a misfit, wasn't he?'
she mused. More than a misfit: restless, insular, detached. And rather wild. She smiled ruefully, thinking
what a tempting recipe that had been for the girls of
Widecombe village!

'Remember when they called him gippo at school?'
John said.

She winced at the reference to István's dark, gypsy
looks. More evidence, she'd once romantically imagined,
that he must be a changeling! Nonsense, of course, given
their parents, but he was so...so totally *dissimilar* in
looks and character.

'Oh, yes. I remember. They only tried that once!' she reminded her brother wryly. 'What an awful fight broke out! István in full attack was frightening to behold!'

'He's got a temper on him like a mad dog with gout.' John grimaced. 'Hell, why do we always discuss the bastard? What about you? How's business?'

The extravagant bow of her mouth extended to form a rueful smile. 'Rough,' she admitted. 'Everyone's hanging on to whatever money they've got—and riding holidays in France don't figure in their budgets. But I'm hopeful about this possible deal with the boss of your hotel. If I can get my prices low enough—and you say the cost of living is relatively cheap here—then I'm in with a fighting chance.'

'You wouldn't need to be struggling and I wouldn't have had to borrow from you if István hadn't bled Mother dry,' grumbled John. He hurled her luggage in the boot of his hire car. 'I don't ever want to see him for the rest of my life. If he ever comes near Lisa, I swear I'll kill him!' He slid into the driver's seat and settled her in. 'I'm scared, hon,' he muttered, staring blankly ahead.

She felt the chill of premonition spread down her spine. So was she. 'Marriage isn't *that* bad!' she said, giving him a diversionary punch.

'I mean I'm scared of István. You know how he and Lisa went around together.' John cleared his throat, fighting for the words while his fingers drummed a tattoo on the steering-wheel and then stilled. 'I'm afraid of comparisons... afraid that... that Lisa will——'

'*No!*' Tanya said forcibly, with a conviction she didn't feel. 'Don't be a dimbo! Good grief, Lisa's letters were *filled* with tedious descriptions,' she cried, forcing a sisterly teasing, 'of you two wandering the streets of Budapest and standing on the Chain Bridge holding hands in the moonlight. She loves you, John! Only a woman in love could write that stuff!'

But, thought Tanya, as the reassured John beamed and launched into an enthusiastic description of how happy he felt, how wonderful, how beautiful, how unique Lisa was, what would happen if Lisa *did* have the opportunity to match steady, stolid John against the devastatingly handsome, devil-may-care István?

Lisa had loved him once so deeply that she...

Tanya bit her lip while John rambled on. She was being crazy. Lisa and John had been engaged for nine months, long enough for any doubts to have crept in by now.

Beyond the Budapest ring road, the arrow-straight motorway took them through lush countryside and Tanya did her best to unwind and enjoy the glorious autumn colours. Eventually they left the motorway and travelled on country lanes. The sharp smell of woodsmoke focused her attention on a village they were now passing through where a stork's nest graced the top of a telegraph pole, flower borders edged the wide street and the water pumps had been painted a bright sky-blue.

'Kastély Huszár,' said John proudly, naming the hotel where he worked as manager.

Ahead, instead of the castle with turrets she'd expected, she saw a grand, eighteenth-century mansion, its steep roof and small turrets set picturesquely against a backdrop of butter-yellow beech woods.

'Wow! Impressive!' she said admiringly, and leant forward as John drove through a pair of fancy wrought-iron gates. 'Pretty classy! They trust you to manage *this*?' she teased.

'I was a bit amazed when I got the job,' he grinned. 'Oh, look, Tan, there's Lisa——'

The car screeched to a stop as John's foot slammed on the brakes. Tanya's body jerked painfully against the seatbelt but she hardly noticed. Shock, hatred—she wasn't sure which—had already slammed the breath from her lungs.

Beside the diminutive, blonde-headed Lisa on the stone stairway that swept to the drive, for all the world as if he were the lord of the manor, stood the unmistakable saturnine figure of their elder brother István. Tanya felt her muscles tighten and suddenly she had the extraordinary urge to jump out of the car and run as far as she could in the opposite direction.

But, 'Drive on,' she grated through her teeth. '*Drive on!*'

'Oh, God! What's he been doing with Lisa?' John shakily put the car in gear and it shuddered forwards.

Dreading the answer to that question, she flicked an anxious glance at his cold, pale face. It mirrored her own fears but she wouldn't help the situation if she let on how worried she was.

'Finding out how deliriously happy she is about marrying you, I expect,' she said firmly. 'Nothing to worry about. Keep calm.' Her aim was to convince herself as much as her younger brother. 'He's history. You and Lisa love one another. He can't touch that.' She prayed that were true. And quailed at the havoc István could wreak. Chaos followed in his tracks as sure as night followed day.

'He'd better not! Do me a favour: keep him occupied while I talk to Lisa and see what's going on,' muttered John.

'Me?' Her mouth opened in dismay. She'd sworn never to speak to István again. She hated him. Yet John's face was so stricken that she knew she had to agree. 'OK,' she said quietly. 'Leave him to me.'

'Look at her! I've never seen her so excited!' hissed John.

'Why shouldn't she be? She *is* getting married to you tomorrow!' Tanya said huskily. Her explanation sounded hollow. Lisa was dancing about, her eyes shining with ... happiness? Exhilaration?

She pressed her icy fingers to the bridge of her nose where a headachy pulse was beginning to throb. István looked so contained, so impregnable as he waited motionless beside the gleefully bouncing Lisa that the prospect of spending any time with him at all was utterly daunting. But she'd do it for John, for the sake of his marriage and for the sake of her dear friend's happiness.

Her legs trembled and she paused to steady herself before she left the car. She'd taken too long, however. The door was opened and István was hauling her out bodily as though she were still his kid sister, paying no attention to the fact that she was now a woman of twenty-four and perfectly capable of manoeuvring her aged body out of a car on her own.

'Welcome,' he murmured, hands of iron firmly under her armpits as he lifted her into the air till she hovered helplessly above his cynical dark face. 'You're quite a woman!' he declared admiringly.

Seething at the insult to her dignity, she kept her expression blank and tried not to let his piercing black eyes unsettle her as he slowly, insolently, assessed the changes that the four years had brought to her appearance.

'Please,' she protested, slanting her eyes anxiously to where John and Lisa were greeting each other like wary acquaintances. She groaned and looked back to István. 'Put me down!' she said sharply.

Annoyingly, her shoe fell off her dangling foot and for a brief moment her eyes blazed with an unguarded fury at the way he'd deliberately put her at a disadvantage and rattled her composure. He had no right to handle her with such familiarity!

'Temper's still simmering away under the haughty exterior, I see,' he observed in an infuriatingly sardonic drawl.

'It's not surprising!' she grated. 'Do you honestly imagine that you can cause pain to my entire family and be welcomed as though nothing had happened?' She felt her anger threatening to escape from way down inside her and ruthlessly clamped irons on it. 'For heaven's sake, put me down!' she ordered. 'I'm not a Barbie doll—or one of your doe-eyed bimbos!'

He did so, slowly, his eyes challenging hers with an unnerving amusement as though he had some dreadful plan in store for her. She responded with an icy glare back, trying to balance on one rather shaky leg. And all the while she was uncomfortably aware that her heart was thudding crazily with a frightening excitement. It seemed, she thought hazily, that she actually relished the thought of tangling in a battle royal with her devilish brother. For a vicar's daughter, that wasn't seemly!

'Allow me,' he murmured, reaching out for her shoe and bending down to ease it on to her foot. 'Hmm. You don't get *these* in a charity shop,' he said from a crouching position, capturing her foot and caressing the leather thoughtfully.

Oh, yes, you do! she thought in amusement. The suit, too. 'An 'impress John's boss' purchase. But her gravity seemed to be faulty and she was forced to place one nervous hand on his shoulder. Just as well she did. The realisation that its width was all him and not padding as she'd imagined seemed to disconcert her. There was a lot more of him, muscle-wise, than when he'd left—and he'd been pretty well-built even then. She wobbled. 'So?'

He smiled faintly. 'Since I know you've hardly two pennies to rub together——'

'Who said?' she interrupted, bristling.

'Lisa.' He smiled again, when she gritted her teeth to conceal her involuntary groan of dismay.

'You've been chatting,' she said flatly.

'Among other things. She told me that you lent John the money to come over here and to keep himself for a few weeks while he looked for work. I gather it left you a bit short. I hope you haven't got into debt.'

'No.' She had intended to leave it there but his lifted eyebrow suggested he was waiting for an explanation. So she gave him one. 'A man was generous to me,' she said, thinking of the elderly manager of the charity shop in Exeter who'd let her have a reduction on the outfit. And then she wondered why she wanted István to believe that men trailed after her as eagerly as women crawled after *him*. In actual fact she'd been too busy to do more than occasionally go out with old schoolfriends who still lived locally. No, not too busy... lacking in interest.

'Serious affair, is it?' he murmured.

It was serious that she, someone who longed to be a mother one day, had no interest in becoming anyone's wife. 'Very,' she answered soberly. 'Didn't Lisa tell you?'

István's thick black eyebrows drew together in disapproval as though news of her affair annoyed him, anger tugging down the corners of his mouth and tightening the strong lines of his jaw. 'No, she didn't. I must admit, I'm surprised any man's got past the impressive defence works.'

Tempted initially to grab a fistful of his raven-silk hair, she glared down at the top of his head and felt a ridiculous urge to stroke it instead. Then, inexplicably, came a fear of touching him at all. He seemed much more *male* than before, and she frowned at the discovery.

'The drawbridge does get let down on occasions,' she said with a shrug.

His long black lashes fluttered then lifted to reveal his wicked, probing glance. His fingers rested briefly on the sheer stockings her father had bought for her and she quivered indignantly at his touch. 'Extravagant... Do hope you stung him for some decent underwear too,' István purred.

The blush stained her face before she could even think of stopping it. 'What an extraordinary thing to say!' she cried in surprise. 'That's hardly the kind of question my brother should be asking!' she added in reproof.

'I agree,' he said with suspicious amiability. 'You're so right. Not brotherly at all, was it?' He paused, contemplating her with a huge grin on his face. That secret again! she thought, intrigued. 'Only underwear salesmen or lovers speak of silk knickers, stocking-tops and black lace bras in low, passionate voices.' His eyes mocked her disapproving expression. 'I know, I know,' he murmured. 'It's very improper for any brother of yours to be concerned with what lies hidden beneath that blue linen barrier. Perhaps,' he suggested in wide-eyed innocence, 'I'm not your brother after all.'

'Some hopes!' she said bitterly. 'I see the same arrogant bully, the same sardonic face, I hear the same cynical cruelty in your voice and I feel ashamed we have the same blood. You're no different. Unfortunately.'

'I think you'll find I've changed,' he said enigmatically.

'Hope springs eternal. Now return my foot,' she said icily, finding his touch on her leg highly disturbing. What was it that bothered her about him? she puzzled. 'I came here to see Lisa, not to stand around like a stork.'

István studied her impassively for a moment, his fingers absently caressing her ankle, and she mused that he must have powerful thigh muscles to stay crouched in that position for so long. A small shiver curled through her, though she wasn't cold.

'You have nicer feet than a stork,' he remarked idly. 'Smoother, sexier——'

'István!' she protested.

He smiled and released her foot, slowly uncurling his body till he was towering over her again. 'Takes you back, doesn't it?' he mused. 'Me, unbuttoning your little Noddy slippers at bedtime, singing some nonsense rhyme——'

'That's quite enough!' she husked, hastily interrupting his reminiscences.

She had no wish to remember. István had won their childhood adoration by singing throaty lullabies in a funny language they thought he'd made up. It had been Hungarian, of course. Why their mother should have taught him to speak her native tongue and him alone, she could never fathom. They were all half Hungarian, after all, but their mother had spoken of her background to no one but István. The rest of them she'd discouraged whenever they'd shown any interest in her homeland. Favouritism, she sighed to herself. It still rankled—and she still felt ashamed that it did.

She had an overwhelming sensation of being crowded by him, and moved back a step to lean against the car. Her eyes slanted to see if John was ready to take her inside. To her alarm, she saw that he and Lisa appeared to be arguing. Adding to her anxiety, István placed both his hands on the car either side of her and leaned forwards in what might have been a friendly intimacy but had the effect of seeming rather unnerving because she was effectively trapped.

'I wanted to remind you of the good times,' he said softly.

'There weren't many—and they were totally overwhelmed by the bad times,' she muttered, shrinking back. 'Why remind us of things we'd rather forget?'

'I'm trying to prepare you,' he said enigmatically.

'For what?' she asked with deep suspicion.

'Changes,' he said silkily. 'Interested?'

She scowled. Fascinated! 'In you?' she fended.

'I thought you might be,' he said lazily. 'From the moment you could toddle, you were jealous of the secrets I shared with Ester,' he added, using their mother's first name as he always had.

'None of us liked you closeted with Mother for two hours every single day,' she said coldly. 'What *were* you doing exactly?'

'Playing music, talking.'

So intently, she thought resentfully, that once when she'd fallen over and had wanted her mother's arms around her she'd had to bang on the locked door for ages before her mother had finally heard her piteous cries. She'd always been second-best. István had come first, everyone else a long way behind. That had hurt.

'Look, István,' she said huskily, 'You must have some idea of the furore you caused when you disappeared and what you did to our family. This is a happy occasion and we don't want any gatecrashers——'

'I was invited,' he said surprisingly and moved back a little, giving Tanya air space at last. 'Isn't that right, Lisa?' he called out. 'Didn't you invite me?'

Tanya flung an appalled glance at her apologetic, guilty-looking friend, who broke away from what looked alarmingly like a full-scale argument with John and ran over to hug her tightly. 'Oh, Lisa,' Tanya said, feeling emotional. 'It's wonderful to see you again, but... what on earth are you doing asking *him* here?' she groaned.

'Wait and see. *Please* keep István occupied as long as you can,' whispered her friend. 'I'm persuading John not to thump him!' She beamed at István encouragingly and hurried back to placate the thunderous John.

Tanya reflectively ticked off three unnerving facts. Lisa glowed. István was trying to hide a self-satisfied smirk. And he was definitely concealing a secret that Lisa knew about. The omens weren't good.

'Whether you had an invitation or not, you should have stayed away,' she muttered, her face pinched with anxiety as Lisa drew John further and further away, out of earshot. The prospect of a long bath and a cup of tea was receding rapidly—but she'd put up with discomfort while John's happiness was at risk. 'It's hypocritical of you to come. What do you care about weddings?'

'I've developed a sudden craving for them,' drawled István.

'You liar!' she retorted. 'Father was right. You just enjoy making trouble, seeing people squirm——'

'No, Tanya,' he growled, a hard glitter in his eyes. 'When he said that, he was being unreasonable. He wasn't entirely rational where I was concerned.'

Tanya took a deep, steadying breath. 'Rational? What was rational about Mother's determination to give you everything and the rest of us nothing? What do you think it did to him, when you got brand new riding boots and we were all hunting for clothes in jumble sales?'

The dangerous glint she'd seen in István's black eyes was extinguished as his lashes swept down to conceal whatever he was thinking. 'It was... difficult, I appreciate that——'

'Not difficult. Impossible!' she bit. He didn't understand. She'd have to be more specific. 'Maybe you *were* the first child, the first-born son; maybe there *is* some archaic Hungarian custom that obliged Mother to empty the contents of her whole purse into your piggy bank, but by golly we got resentful, and no wonder!' she said bitterly.

'My education must have cost a great deal,' he agreed quietly, his eyes on her like a watchful hawk.

'Vast sums,' she said unhappily. 'Lavished exclusively on you. No wonder we were poor. Mother even quarrelled with Father about the way she spent her money!'

'I know. I heard them. Did you ever wonder where Ester got so much money from?' he enquired idly.

'She brought it with her when she escaped from Communist Hungary as a young woman,' she snapped.

'And worked as a daily help in the vicarage. It's a strange thing to do, when you have such savings, isn't it?' he murmured.

Tanya frowned. She'd never thought of that before. 'She—she always liked to be busy——'

'Another thing. She never spent the money on herself at all. The only person she gave it to was me. Odder still, wouldn't you say?'

'Unfair! What are you trying to tell me?' she asked warily, unsettled by the inconsistencies of her mother's behaviour.

'To think beyond your resentment. A sense of injustice has robbed you of your brains. Was the money so important to you?' he probed.

'No! The injustice, like you said!' she muttered. 'And the fact that Mother was besotted with you to the exclusion of the rest of us.'

'Besotted?' His eyebrow arched in disagreement. 'Did she hug me? Kiss me as much as she kissed you and John and your sisters?'

She frowned at the detached way he'd spoken about them all, as if he was talking about someone else's family. In a way that was true. Her father had disowned him. 'Of course she...' Her voice lost its initial confidence and her frown deepened as she struggled in vain to recall any moment of affection between her mother and István. 'No,' she said slowly. 'No, she didn't! In fact...I can

hardly remember her cuddling you at all!' Her
amazement apparently pleased him. Something made her
think that he was coaxing her towards some extraordinary conclusion.

'Curiouser and curiouser!' murmured István.

'Not particularly,' Tanya retorted quickly, loyal in
defending her mother's behaviour. It had been strange,
though. What their mother had felt for István was an
unusual kind of love. Nearer to a slavish devotion. 'No
hugs,' she mused, after a moment. And felt sorry for
him.

'Why do you think that was?' he queried.

Her huge eyes lifted to his, catching a glimpse of the
raw emotion he was obviously feeling. No hugs. Her
understanding of his character deepened. 'I don't know,
it's inexplicable. Mother was a warm and loving woman
to the rest of us. I can't...' She wrestled with the discovery. 'Perhaps you weren't the cuddly sort,' she
suggested feebly.

'Not everyone was of that opinion,' he said softly. His
eyes were fixed intently on her, but almost immediately
they swivelled to where Lisa stood pleading with John.

Tanya froze. The implication was all too plain. Lisa
had once found him eminently huggable. 'I hope you're
not here to make trouble,' she breathed, alarmed to see
a slow, sensual smile of wicked promise curve his lips.
'Are you?' she demanded.

'All I've done is to turn up for a family wedding,' he
said with disarming innocence.

'You can cause trouble even when you're not around!'
she complained.

His dark gaze swept back to fasten on her accusing
eyes. 'Meaning?'

'Like when you never turned up for meals, or never
came home at night,' she said in a low tone. 'Don't you
know how upset Mother was? We stayed up all hours,
waiting for you——'

'So you were worried!' he husked.

Drat him, how did he work that one out? Her tone, probably, she thought morosely. She'd betrayed the anxiety she'd felt. The last thing she wanted was for István to know she'd idolised him!

Happiness had once been doing anything that her elder brother did. Like a fool, she'd trailed all over the moors, fifty careful yards behind him, the victim of her own hero-worship. She'd fished the same river, had ridden to the same rocky crag. But then her riding lessons had been cancelled, she remembered with a sigh. Hell hath no fury like a thirteen-year-old girl denied her pony!

Worse, he'd stopped tolerating her quiet adoration and had begun to snap and snarl at her as though she irritated him. The early, childhood days of affection changed almost overnight to a bad-tempered rejection. Her own brother didn't want to be bothered with her any more and pride had made her pretend she didn't care.

'Me? Worried about you? Good grief,' she said lightly, 'I'm well aware that the Devil looks after his own. I stayed up to keep Mother company,' she added, skirting around the truth.

She knew only too painfully what her mother must have been feeling when István failed to turn up. A deep, searing anxiety that was as intense as a physical pain. He could have been lying somewhere in a ditch after falling off his motorbike. Concussed from being thrown by his horse. Drowned in the river. Even now it angered her to think of the needless hours of worry.

'All those times when you rolled in without an explanation or an apology,' she continued, 'I could never fathom why Mother put up with your thoughtlessness, why she always welcomed you back with open arms and a mug of cocoa and digestive biscuits!' she finished crossly.

'Well, she understood me better than the rest of you,' he said with a slight shrug of his big shoulders. 'She knew what I was doing and that I could take care of myself. And that there were times when I had to get out and roam the moors or drive till I was exhausted. I can't stand being fenced in. Don't you know that by now? I need a free rein——'

'Freedom!' She fought back the angry tears, struggled to crush the hurtful memories and lashed out blindly. 'How can you say you were fenced in? You had all the freedom you wanted! You were spoilt rotten!' she seethed. 'And you gave *nothing* back but heartache!' Flinging a hasty glance in John's direction, she saw he was well out of earshot and recklessly let her tongue take her further. 'You seduced Lisa!' she hissed. 'You put her life in danger. You——'

'Yes? Go on,' he goaded, his eyes glittering. 'Say it.'

Her teeth ground together, preventing the hot spurt of angry words. If she spoke of the time Lisa lost István's baby, she knew she'd howl her eyes out because she was on the brink of losing control of her emotions. He'd been twenty-four and should have known better. Lisa, nineteen, almost three months pregnant. Tanya's body trembled.

'You never showed an ounce of family feeling!' she grated, chickening out of the direct accusation. 'That's why I fail to see why you've come here at this time. You're not here to celebrate the wedding, are you? You and John have always loathed each other.' That left Lisa as the reason, she thought in dismay. Her voice rose half an octave. 'What...what *did* make you turn up here?'

'I decided I had to make a play for what I wanted,' he said softly.

Her heart thudded. 'That's what I was afraid of!' she said jerkily. 'István——'

'Pleading will do no good. My mind is made up.' He looked at her steadily. 'I refuse to be rushed by you, or anyone. I'm very much my own man, Tanya. I'm calling the shots and in time all will be revealed,' he drawled, and turned to go.

'Running away again?' she taunted, half out of her mind with despair at his intentions. He froze and she knew she'd actually reached a vulnerable part of that apparently impenetrable skin. It gave her no pleasure, however. Somehow he always turned her into a shrew—and that was awful. She hated herself for complaining and whinging, for letting her raw emotions bubble to the surface, for being bitchy. He made her feel less good about herself. That was why she hated to be near him.

Slowly he turned and walked towards her again. 'I didn't run,' he interrupted, a thinly disguised anger underlying the soft tones. 'I left of my own choice. Why don't you say it, Tanya? Say what you must and get it out of your system.'

She took a deep breath, the pain swelling to the surface while she struggled with the souring hurt that had destroyed her happiness. 'All right. You claim that you left?' she echoed bitterly, blurting it all out in a spurt of spitting flame. 'Call it what you like, blame who you like; you went without warning, without leaving any address—and—and—you—drove Mother into her grave and—and for that I'll never, *ever* forgive you!'

He remained motionless. Her heart rolled over in sickening lurches because she'd voiced the words that had become engraved on her heart and because she had finally faced him with one truth after all the years of nursing its canker inside her.

István's eyes flashed dangerously. 'How could I kill her?' he growled. 'I was in Budapest at the time.'

'But she didn't know that! You were special to her and you'd vanished without trace. She went into a decline. Soon after, she died. Isn't the connection obvious?' she asked huskily.

Waves of remembered distress made the muscles in her stomach clench as if a ruthless hand gripped her there. A sob lurched from her tremulous lips. Her pained eyes lifted to his and saw . . . pity.

'Tan,' he began, tight with strain.

'No! Don't look at me like that! I don't want it! It's too late to show sympathy!' she cried hoarsely. 'What do you care that Mother was beside herself because you'd vanished?'

'What did I care?' he roared. And suddenly, his eyes burning with an intense light, he grabbed her arms in an explosion of movement, his teeth bared in a furious snarl as he shook her violently. 'What the hell do you know about me?' he seethed.

Nothing, that was the pity of it all, she thought in silent answer before her brain stopped functioning. Pain erupted in her head, her bruised arms, her neck where it snapped back and forth. 'István, István!' she gasped above the roaring in her ears.

Mercifully he came to his senses and held her steady. Her shocked, accusing eyes lifted and widened at the pallor and the gauntness of his face. 'Twenty-seven years...' he muttered through bloodless lips. 'And of all the women I have to vent my frustration on I choose you.'

So he wanted to hurt her. Hearing him, the once-adored elder brother, coldly admitting that he was targeting her was unbearable. Her resolve to be remote and unemotional collapsed under the weight of her own terrible emptiness.

To her total dismay, hot tears overflowed from her stricken eyes and emptied in scalding torrents down her cheeks. With a harsh exclamation, he growled some words in Hungarian then bewildered her by gathering her in his arms and holding her tightly in a bear-hug. The embrace was so welcome, so comfortable and so achingly familiar that she sobbed even harder.

'I know how much you loved Ester. You did your best to love us all,' he stated in a harsh mutter. Her shoulders shook and he stroked them. 'You're so like her. Strong sense of duty. Loyal. Dogged in your determination and totally blind to anything but what you have to do, like a blinkered horse.'

He was absently stroking the chestnut river of her hair and speaking to her in the same kind of voice he'd once used when she was small and needed comfort in those far-off and innocent days before he'd taken an inexplicable dislike to her. Longing for that time again and disturbed by his gentleness, she buried her face deeper into his warm chest.

Shame filled her. It was a shame brought on by the realisation that the death of her beloved mother had been as traumatic an event as István's disappearance. That shouldn't be. He didn't deserve her regrets. Missing her mother dreadfully, she'd missed István just as much. Two people she'd loved profoundly had gone from her life with a shattering finality.

'Hush, Tan. I'm here.'

Desperately she tried not to cry. When her mother had died, she hadn't shed one tear. Her sisters had been inconsolable and she'd cuddled them in her arms till they'd fallen asleep but she'd remained cold, her feelings frozen.

Her hands curled against István's chest. Safely in her wallet were pictures of him and her mother which comforted her somehow to know that they were there. She could touch the wallet and project her passionate hatred of him to wherever he was in the world. And now he was here and she was in his arms and feeling as if she'd come home. It was all wrong!

István's strong hand lifted her chin and he stared deeply into her eyes while gently wiping her face with his handkerchief. 'I'm glad you've cried,' he said huskily. 'I heard you'd never shed a tear.' His hand faltered. There was a softening of his mouth that disturbed her, a light in his eyes she hadn't seen before. 'You're more ethereal than ever. I've never seen you look more beautiful, Tanya,' he breathed, a frightening hunger in his voice.

Her throat dried. Beneath the pale suit, her breasts rose and fell with the shallow breath that sought in vain to oxygenate her depleted body. He had an animal magnetism, an intense sexuality that even she, his sister, could feel. Lisa would be a pushover to that unholy, electrical force emanating from him. With barely a thought for the consequences, he switched it on and flooded anyone in his path in a dazzling display of male power.

The blood began to drum in her veins. She couldn't have moved if her life had depended on it. He held her gaze with the sheer force of his personality and all she could do was to stare at the incredibly sexy mouth and wonder...

Oh, dear heaven! she thought in horror. What *is* it about István?

And he told her.

'I feel it too,' he growled softly.

'Feel...what?' she croaked in a revealingly high-pitched voice.

István breathed heavily a few times before elaborating, his wicked black eyes relentless. 'Desire.'

'What are you saying...? *No!*' she whispered in horror, her mouth only just managing to shape the denial as he moved forwards to close the gap between them. 'No, István!'

But her speech was slurred and he smiled in triumph. 'Poor Tanya,' he said soothingly, his warm breath torching across her face. 'I think I'd better put you out of your misery.'

Her skin prickled with tension. 'You're depraved! Heaven help you, István!' she rasped, her voice shaking with raw emotion. 'Your mind is twisted. I wish we weren't related! If only there were no ties between us—and never had been! I wish—oh, dear God, I wish you'd never been born and that you weren't my brother!'

'That last wish is granted,' he said silkily, dropping a light kiss on her parched lips. 'I'm not.'

'What?' she croaked, bewildered. And all the time she was thinking, No, no! No, it can't be true...

'I'm not your brother.' There was something terrible in the depths of his eyes but his tone was light-hearted. 'Opens up all sorts of possibilities, doesn't it?'

CHAPTER TWO

TANYA'S senses reeled. For a moment she didn't grasp what he was saying and then the full impact of his statement hit her. And by then he was halfway up the castle steps. Numbly, paralysed with shock, she watched his tall, lithe figure in the woman-baiting white shirt and tight black jeans disappear into the hotel.

But it wasn't true. It was impossible. He'd made a cruel joke to torment her.

She would have run after him if she could move. She would yell at him to leave them all alone if she could succeed in pushing her voice past the awful lump that blocked her throat. Not her brother—a terrible thing to say—a slur on her parents' integrity!

And yet...

Voices impinged on her consciousness. John's bitter anger, Lisa's agitated wails. Her entire body trembled with anger as it dawned on her that István was set fair to ruin the fairy-tale wedding they'd all planned for and had looked forward to with such excitement.

John's needs fought with her own. His had a greater priority and her instincts were always to respond to her family's needs. Grimly she forced herself to dismiss István's outrageous claim as pure, wicked fantasy and to contain her own chaotic feelings. István she could deal with later. This was infinitely more urgent, though at the moment she wasn't sure whether she should break up the argument or let it blow itself out. Curse István! She scowled, hating to see her brother so upset.

As for that dizzy sensation she'd felt . . . She was tired. Getting her father comfortably settled, cooking masses of meals for him and freezing them, watering the plants, worrying about leaving him and then worrying even more about Lisa's love for John—all this had tired her emotionally and physically.

Someone spoke to her. A young woman, dressed entirely in black and carrying a basket of freshly baked bread that smelled deliciously warm and doughy. Tanya registered hunger as she absently returned the woman's greeting and it suddenly became clear that much of her confused thinking had also been due to her early start that morning without a proper breakfast.

A wry smile touched her pale lips. Hunger pangs, mimicking sexual desire! And then her smile faded as she realised more fully what István had said. He'd casually disowned the mother who'd devoted her life to him. He deserved nothing but contempt for his behaviour. Her hands shaped into fists.

'Not your brother.' Ridiculous! Her mother would have told her if he'd been adopted... Wouldn't she? At the very least, her father would have said something when István had vanished. Bitterness and resentment would have drawn such a fact out of her father, surely? Or he would have told her recently in one of those long, companionable heart-to-hearts.

Crushing the rebellious nagging doubts that kept whispering slyly in her ear, she marshalled her thoughts together. At the moment, Lisa and John needed her. Making sure their wedding went ahead was the most important thing on the agenda and anything that was between herself and István could wait—*must* wait.

'Here goes,' she muttered, heading towards John and Lisa. Ignore István, she told herself. Think only of the wedding. But smiling was more difficult than she'd hoped.

'Are you going to show me this hotel of yours or am I camping out here?' she asked John jokingly in a rather stiff little voice that went with the rigid smile.

'Sorry, I——' began John.

'You and István didn't get on,' sighed Lisa despondently, slumped rather inappropriately against a statue of Cupid. 'I heard you arguing.'

Tanya looked at her anxiously. Now István was gone, the light had left Lisa's face. 'Good grief! He and I will always be at daggers drawn!' she said lightly. 'That doesn't matter a scrap. Pretend he's not here. I'm dying to hear all the arrangements. Can you take my luggage, John?'

Conscious of the need to reassure Lisa, to remind her friend that John was reliable and steady and loved her, she tucked her arm in Lisa's, pushing her towards the hotel steps. John remained stony-faced as he stalked along beside them so she sought ways to break the deadlock between them and lift the funereal atmosphere.

'It's thrilling that you two are crazy about each other!' she continued warmly. Was that overkill? she wondered. 'All that gush in your letters, you old romantic! The lights on the Danube, the candlelit dinners...isn't it just great that you're marrying my kid bro?'

'Great,' said Lisa dutifully.

Tanya hid a wail of despair. She'd sounded less than overjoyed. As if...as if her mind was elsewhere. 'So, what's the plan? I thought I'd go to my room and unpack first,' she continued, managing to sound quite cheerful. Poor John, she thought miserably. He looked ashen. She must act, act, *act*! 'Then I'll do us all a favour and get rid of the wretched You-Know-Who. I thought an acid bath might do the trick, John!' she joked.

'I'll empty a few car batteries,' he muttered, his eyes dark with worry.

Tanya tried to give a tinkle of laughter but it wasn't too convincing. She knew instinctively that he and Lisa would argue again when they were alone. And somewhere in the hotel, with any luck, she'd be throwing crockery at the incorrigible István. Some family reunion, she thought morosely.

'If I'm not camping under the stars, I suppose you've put me in some dark cellar!' she said with painful brightness.

'Got it in one. The best cellar we have, on the first floor. Lisa's next door in the bridal-suite cellar,' John jokingly answered, rallying himself with an effort and forcing a faint, brave smile.

'Lovely,' Tanya enthused, scanning the big windows above. A figure in white moved away quickly, as though the person didn't want to be seen. Not István, someone smaller. Probably a curious maid, she thought dismissively.

And, as they walked up the steps with John trying for *her* sake to be normal and talking about the range of facilities at the castle hotel, Tanya saw that Lisa's eyes were searching for something or someone and she knew who it must be.

István.

She quailed. He still dominated their lives, even in his absence. It was quite plain that Lisa felt his magnetism far too strongly for a woman on the brink of marrying someone else. Poor John! mourned Tanya. He'd adored Lisa from the very first and had resented any time that Lisa had spent with István. John had tried desperately to drag himself out of his elder brother's giant shadow—without success. Who could? Shadows were elusive, impossible to pin down. Impossible to hurt, too.

'. . . here in the old hall,' John was saying with quiet pride.

Guiltily, she pulled herself together and looked around the high-ceilinged room, genuinely delighted to see that it looked like the interior of an exquisite eighteenth-century mansion, with none of the usual trappings of a hotel.

'John!' she cried warmly, admiring the mirrored walls. 'I'm quite staggered! How clever of you to get a job here! It's absolutely beautiful—especially the flower displays and romantic garlands. And look at this furniture! By golly,' she added in awe, 'it's all antiques!'

'Every stick,' nodded John. 'It was all inherited by the countess, my boss.'

'I'm surprised this stuff wasn't looted and transported back to Moscow during the Communist Occupation,' mused Tanya.

Her brother smiled absently. 'Perhaps she hid it. She's a very astute and nice lady. You'll like her when we get together to talk about the riding school. She lives on the estate.' His smile turned to a frown. Lisa was rather obviously searching for István. 'I'll get the key and sign you in,' he ground out tightly, reining in his temper.

Tanya waited till he'd reached an antique desk before she took the bull by the horns and rounded on her miserable-looking friend. 'Lisa, I don't know what you're doing, but you're hurting John!' she whispered in exasperation. 'Can't you ignore István even for one moment?'

'Can you?' retorted Lisa.

'No-*yes*!' Tanya heaved an impatient sigh. 'You're confusing me,' she muttered. 'How long's István been here?'

'So you are interested in me,' came his satin-smooth voice just behind her and suddenly there were two dozen Istváns in the hall with them, dark, menacing and devilishly handsome from every angle.

'Only as a porter,' said Tanya crisply, annoyed that Lisa had abandoned her and crept away to John's side—and because her pulses had inexplicably leapt into life. The reason for that was so unthinkable that she dismissed it out of hand.

'A porter? Doesn't seem to be one around. Must be a coffee-break,' said István, unperturbed by her put-down. 'How cool you are. What control!' he said in admiration. 'Don't you have one or two burning questions to ask me?'

Millions, she thought—but not with John and Lisa around. Ignoring him then, she pretended to be surveying the lovely wedding swags and garlands that hung everywhere.

'Admiring the orchids?' he enquired softly.

The flowers registered more fully on her conscious mind. Her head jerked up. 'Orchids!' she exclaimed sadly.

An ache weighed down her heart. Poignant memories were associated with the bouquet of white orchids that István had sent for their mother's funeral. Her father had thrown the flowers in the dustbin and so István's tribute had never taken their rightful place on her mother's coffin. That fact had deeply distressed her.

'Ester's favourite flowers,' ruminated István quietly, apparently unaware of the drama inside her head.

'I know,' she said huskily. He'd been the only one to remember. He'd always given her mother orchids on her birthday. She'd once said that they reminded her of the ones that had been grown in the hothouse close to her old home in Hungary.

István touched her shoulder to regain her attention because she'd averted her face from his. No way did she want him to know how close she was to tears.

'Tell me something,' he said gently. 'What do you think of Kastély Huszár? Intimidating? Alien? Not to your taste, perhaps?'

Glad he'd turned to more mundane things, she eyed him scornfully. If he was trying to play down the attractions of John's hotel, he'd find her unresponsive. 'Friendly, welcoming and quite the loveliest place I've ever seen,' she answered, warmth seeping into her tone. 'Hasn't John done well?'

'Oh, he's landed himself a good job all right,' admitted István.

'I'm glad you realise it,' she said drily.

'I'm glad *you* do. I want you to be quite aware of his good fortune.'

Her forehead wrinkled with a puzzled frown. 'I imagine all these deep, meaningful remarks are leading somewhere?'

'I hope so,' he said silkily, his sensual mouth quivering with amusement. 'I sincerely do hope so.'

It was as if he wanted her to find him seductive, she thought dazedly. And blinked. Alarmed, she said the first thing that came into her head. 'I do think he's organised the foyer well,' she burbled. 'A shiny reception desk with pigeon-holes for keys and people in uniform and badges would have been out of place. With those books and hats and things scattered about, it's like someone's home.' Mercifully she ran out of breath.

'Home? Not like our home used to be, I hope. There'll be tears before bedtime, if so,' he said enigmatically.

Tanya stiffened. 'What precisely do you mean by that?' she demanded, her eyes dark and wary.

'I'm talking from my own point of view, of course,' he replied smoothly. 'I found the family remarkably divided.'

'You *left* the family divided,' she corrected tartly.

'I'm flattered you imagine it was all my own work,' he drawled sardonically. 'Of course,' he reflected, 'you were incapable of really seeing anyone's faults. Everyone loved *you* because you accepted them, faults and all, and were more concerned for others than yourself. You were the mediator.'

'I was?' she said, surprised. It hadn't been a role she'd been aware of.

'You tried a little too hard to see the best side of each and every one of us and I admired that,' he told her idly. 'Though you gave up on me.'

'Hardly surprising,' she said coldly. Her curiosity got the better of her, though. 'What—what faults did everyone else have—yours being glaringly obvious?'

'Well, despite all your gentle hints, you never managed to modify your mother's odd obsession with me, or to change the fact that your father favoured John far more than you three girls. As for Sue, well, you never curbed her passion for cutting up any clothes left lying around and returning them with every inch re-designed and embroidered. I had a bit of explaining to do at boarding-school when the under-matrons unpacked two shirts with smocking on the front!'

Tanya laughed and then felt guilty that she'd done so. 'Mariann?' she prompted.

He smiled. 'You worried unnecessarily over the fact that she sent out totally unconscious signals to every male within a radius of a hundred miles. You worried that she'd become a fallen woman if you didn't protect her and form a human barrier against the young men who hung around her. I don't suppose it ever occurred to you that they were rather taken with you, too.'

'Of course they weren't!' she said hotly. 'Mariann's got the looks, not me. And yes, it did worry me for her sake, but she seems to take men's admiration in her stride and isn't vain or promiscuous at all.'

Tanya thought that it was extraordinary that he should have noticed so much, because he'd always seemed quite indifferent to family life. Those thumbnail sketches of them all made her feel rather uncomfortable. It was as though he'd watched them from a stranger's viewpoint and judged them with clinical detachment. *Your* mother, he'd said; *your* father. Had that been deliberate or unconscious? All at once, she was beginning to entertain serious doubts about his relationship to her.

'You—you were joking about not being my brother, weren't you?' she asked shakily.

'No.' The word vibrated through her body.

Suddenly she was too scared to believe him. Scared of the way she was beginning to respond, scared of the churning emotions working away inside her, destroying all caution. 'It can't be true! Mother would have told us when she knew she was dying,' she said huskily. 'You're up to something! Why are you here, István?' she asked with passionate intensity. 'Tell me!'

'In time. This is not the moment.' His eyes gleamed. 'When you've been parted from someone and you've both gone your separate ways, you don't rush the reunion. It's too volatile a situation and calls for a more delicate, less impulsive touch.'

She gulped in dismay at the husky threat in his tone. He was admitting that he was playing a cat-and-mouse game and meant slyly to work his way into Lisa's affections again. However, her intended protest was shelved when she realised that John had returned.

'All done?' She smiled wanly. Not long now, perhaps a sharp show-down with István in a moment, and then she could be alone to gather herself together. She put a hand on John's arm affectionately. 'Don't bother to show me my room. Let me have the key. You spend time with Lisa,' she continued, a meaningful look in her eyes, 'while this reprobate with the designer muscles makes himself useful by carrying my case.'

If she did anything, she decided, she'd make sure the bride and groom-to-be sorted out their differences. Meanwhile, once she and István were less in the public eye, she'd insist on knowing what he was doing here. *And* how soon he was going. Perhaps she could help him on his way, she thought grimly, contemplating the toe of her shoe with malicious intent.

'So, the fun begins,' murmured István, swinging the key backwards and forwards.

'With bells on!' she agreed tightly, planning plans.

He picked up her case, and the piece of hand-luggage that she'd nursed throughout the journey, double-stacked them porter-style and imperiously grabbed Tanya's hand. 'Let's go upstairs and ring a few of those bells, then,' he smiled, hauling her across the vast expanse of black and white chequer-board tiles so fast that she had to cling on to him like mad or slip on the glassy surface.

'Let me go, you brute!' she cried, afraid. Afraid of falling. Afraid of the contact. Her skin prickled.

Her hair was coming down in thick chestnut hanks over her shoulders and she was in danger of ricking an ankle if she didn't wrench free. On an impulse, she scooped up a delicate porcelain vase from a glossy fruitwood table and prepared to aim it at István's head.

'You want bells, now hear them ringing!' she fumed.

'Mistake,' he murmured. Because she'd given him time to drop her luggage straight to the floor with not an atom of regard for their contents, grab the vase and unwrap her fingers from it. 'A little over the top, wasn't it?' he enquired smoothly.

She flushed, horrified at what she'd intended. 'A girl has to defend herself from rogue bell-ringers,' she muttered in excuse.

'Sure. But do it some way that doesn't involve one of Napoleon's favourite bits of porcelain,' he said drily.

'His what?' she scoffed. 'Stop this endless make-believe! You can't possibly know anything about the contents of this building! You've only been here... how long is it now?'

'Long enough to know my way around,' he answered, dodging her sly question. 'Hope I haven't broken anything in your cases.' He lifted them and jiggled them around a little. 'Chastity belt, is it?' he asked wickedly, at a rattling sound. 'Dear, oh, dear! What *are* you going to do if it's broken?' And he sauntered on up the stairs, leaving her steaming at his outrageous behaviour.

Since he had her luggage and the key to her room, and—she sighed—since it was up to her to get rid of him somehow she had no alternative but to follow. With the distinct impression that she was dancing to every tune he called, she stomped up the stairs so fast that she managed to draw level with him before he reached the top landing.

'I've got Lisa's present in there!' she said angrily. 'If you've ruined it, you can get a replacement. It cost——' She bit her lip. Far too much, more than she could afford, but she was so thrilled for John and her dear friend. Distressed by his carelessness, she felt crosser than ever. 'You're like a hurricane!' she bit. 'Blasting your way through people's lives, destroying anything in your path. You ruin everything you lay your hands on——'

'I've lain hands on you a few times, heaving you out of the danger you got yourself into, and you look OK,' he observed, giving her a rather insulting once-over. A shiver curled, unbidden, right the way through her body at the smouldering in his dark, bottomless eyes. 'You're all in one piece,' he said in a soft, husky growl, 'all the appropriate bumps in the right places——'

'István!' she protested, knowing she must be pillar-box red by now. Her blushes had even heated through to her loins and that had never happened before. But then no other man had ever shaken her out of her comfortable, ordered world. 'Don't talk like that!' she said crossly.

'I'm trying to wake you up to the truth as gently as possible,' he said mildly.

'No,' she said stubbornly. 'You've *got* to be my brother. Stop tormenting me like this——'

They turned down the long landing and István put an arm around her shoulders. As she shrugged it off irritably, she saw a flutter of a guest's white skirt as a door ahead shut abruptly.

'You're looking a little flushed,' he crooned.

'I'm angry,' she seethed.

'Anger, is it? I thought I might have reached some... soft centre, some responsive core of that gorgeous body.'

She gasped. 'Stop it!' she grated.

'When I do,' he said softly, 'you'll wish I were still talking.'

She stumbled. The evidence was increasingly stacked against the fact that István was her brother. 'Don't *touch* me!' she snapped, when his warm hand steadied her. Her pulses had started a riot all of their own. Some of them had decided to throb in her throat, where he could see them. So she clenched her jaw together and tried desperately not to think of István's beautiful, wicked mouth.

'You'll grind down to the gums if you don't give your feelings some release,' he murmured.

Her almond eyes slanted viciously at his laughing face and away again, hastily. He was too darn handsome! Too arrogant. Too... *impossible*! 'I don't think so,' she said frostily, determined to stop him trying to dent her armour with sly insinuations and outrageous teasing. 'For your information, there's a core of steel all the way through me.'

'Malleable stuff, steel,' he ruminated, nodding towards a medieval breast-plate on the tapestry-hung wall to illustrate his words. 'It's strong and cold to the touch, of course. But build up a fire hot enough underneath it, and when it reaches melting point...' His eyes glimmered. 'Now there's a thought!' he exclaimed. 'Some man could come along and mould you to any shape he wants!'

Irritated by the way he twisted things to his own purpose, she gave a derisive laugh. 'I'm well aware that's what you're trying to do to all of us,' she snapped. 'But this time we're wise to you. If you've come——'

'Maybe I'm a reformed character, come to make my peace,' he said quietly, with a sideways glance at her grim profile.

Her astonished glance caught his and was momentarily trapped before she summoned up enough willpower to look away, unable to withstand the alarmingly intense message of warmth there.

She gave her head a little shake, frantic to dispel the terrible thoughts that crowded her head. Her eyes skimmed the dauntingly broad shoulders, the swell of his chest with its bunched muscles, the narrow hips——

'I ride,' he said suddenly.

Tanya jumped, startled. 'Should I be interested?' she retorted guiltily.

'You were staring at my body,' he said, deceptively as mild as milk. 'I thought you were wondering how I kept fit. Am I mistaken? Were you staring because you feel attracted to me?' he suggested wickedly.

'Of course not!' she cried, hot and bothered by the mere idea. Questions hovered on her lips—were almost blurted out. But a fear held her back. She was afraid to learn that her parents had lived a lie, that her father in particular had betrayed his strict adherence to truth and honesty.

'Well, then.' He smiled and paused, still smiling. If he were a woman, she thought in exasperation, she'd call it a full Mona Lisa effort. An 'I have plans for you' smile. 'As my clothes aren't special enough to fascinate you for the prolonged assessment you were giving me, and since you strenuously deny a sexual interest, your... intent scrutiny,' he said insolently, 'must be because you're wondering if I'm a fitness freak. The answer is that I indulge myself in almost every sport I can,' he told her in a conversational tone. 'I like to keep supple because I need strength and stamina. Perhaps I'd better not tell you what for.'

'No. I'd rather you didn't,' she agreed with enough frost injected in her voice to burn peach-blossom.

Strength, suppleness, stamina. She thought of the ease with which he'd lifted her when they'd met outside the castle and then more wistfully of the occasions in the past when he'd tossed her in the air to banish her tears. He'd barely tolerated her following him on his lonely walks like a devoted puppy. Yet if ever she got stuck in a bog on the moorland or fell into the river he'd always be there, whisking her up, tending to her injuries and heaving her on his shoulder with a half-irritated, half-amused sigh and bearing her back to where her sisters played together, oblivious to her adventures.

But she'd been younger then and it was before his domination of the Evans family had begun in earnest. Which reminded her.

'*Are* you here to make trouble?' she persisted, while he jiggled a heavy iron key in the brass lock of a room labelled 'Madách'.

'Of course!' he said airily, as if that went without saying. 'Ring a few bells, expose old wounds to the air——'

'Break a heart or two,' she ventured apprehensively.

He paused and thought for a moment. 'Break into one, perhaps,' he acknowledged slowly and she felt her spine become a pillar of ice at the thought of the vulnerable Lisa and her dear, lovesick brother. 'You're honoured. I have a feeling this is one of the best rooms in the hotel,' István went on in a conversational tone and opening the door, 'because it's named after a famous writer——'

'Whose heart?' she said huskily, not interested in a lecture on Hungarian notables.

There was a brief silence while he appeared to be considering his words. In placing her cases on the rack provided a raven lock of hair fell on to his high, smooth forehead. Tanya almost reached out to lift it back in an affectionate, sisterly gesture but clenched her fist instead, recognising angrily that he was deliberately spinning out his answer to torment her.

Nervously she strolled around the spacious room, pretending to be admiring the period furniture: the heavy four-poster bed with its fairy-tale stack of duvets and outsize pillows, fit for any Princess and the Pea illustration; the polished floorboards; the expensive white silk drapes at the high floor-length windows. Lavish was the only word that described it all. John's prospects would be wonderful if it weren't for István.

'Whose heart?' she repeated harshly, unable to bear the wait any longer. This was like pulling teeth!

'That rather depends on how many bells I get to ring. Some people,' said István in a voice so rich with sensuality that she was forced to grip the swagged bed-curtains to stop herself from turning around, 'hide their feelings with such success that no one knows whether they're in anguish inside or merely wondering if it's going to rain. Others opt for the danger of total openness——'

'Not you,' she whispered, attempting to control the rapid beat of her pulses by breathing deeply. Odd how nervous she was, she reflected.

'No. Not me,' agreed István, coming to stand inches away from her and sending her pulses haywire again. His eyes glowed as dark and as warm as a black stallion's coat. 'I play my cards close to my chest till I know I can come up trumps.'

Disconcerted, she moved to her cases and flipped them open. 'Some would question whether you had a heart at all,' she muttered.

He'd broken the hearts of their father, mother, Lisa and herself as if no blood, no ties bound them together. Only her sisters, bound up in each other, had been partly protected from István's brutal determination to dominate and crush everyone around him.

'Is it broken?' he enquired softly.

For a moment, fooled by his sympathetic tone, she thought he'd meant her heart. She spun around so fast in alarm that she teetered briefly on her high heels, and he reached out to save her from falling.

'Take your hands off me!' she rasped, horrified by the electric shock that had passed through her. Why? *Why*? she thought frantically.

'OK, I apologise for saving you from landing on your neat little bottom!' he drawled. 'I merely thought you'd want to preserve that oh-so-dignified, nose-in-the-air haughtiness you've acquired. Is it broken?' he murmured. 'Have I...cracked it?'

He was laughing at her! Deep in the molten pools of his damnable eyes she could see glints of amusement! And once again there was a wealth of meaning in his words. More than she could fathom. 'If you mean my present to Lisa, no, it isn't.'

'I'm glad. Want to know what I'm giving her?' he asked with a sinister, lazy drawl.

At the implication, her heart seemed to stop beating and then it roared into life again, double-quick, as a protest. 'No!'

'It's not silk underwear.'

Clenching her teeth, she said through them, 'I should hope not! Stop hinting that you're going to stir up trouble!'

'You used to be so intensely curious. Are you indifferent to what I'm giving Lisa, or afraid I'll say something you don't want to hear?' he asked, satin-smooth.

'Indifferent,' she lied angrily. 'And I should have thought that even you would have had the good taste not to give Lisa and John a present. They won't want to be reminded of you during their marriage. And while we're about it, it's tactless in the extreme for you to lurk about at a time like this—rather like a spectre at a wedding feast!'

Glittering lights danced from under his lowered lashes. 'You think I should leave before I do any harm?'

'Yes,' she bit out.

'Ask me nicely.'

She checked a rude retort. This was her chance to plead on behalf of the young lovers. 'I——' She bit into her full lower lip. The plea stuck in her throat.

'Beg me,' he drawled lazily. 'I'd love to see that pride of yours dented with humility. It might remind you of your more appealing gentleness when you were more——'

'Malleable?' she suggested icily. 'Good grief, István! All you want is for women to be obedient and adoring! Everyone has to play second fiddle to you, don't they? Just because I don't——'

'Follow me like a dog?' he supplied helpfully.

She coloured up angrily, her mouth grim. 'Any flash young man who can do circus tricks on horseback would gather admirers, especially in a sleepy village like Widecombe-in-the-Moor in deepest Devon!' she cried hotly. 'As soon as I learnt discrimination, I realised that anyone who tried to go further than skin-deep with you would find that there wasn't anyone at home!'

'Amusing, acerbic, bitchy. Quite a change from the Tanya I knew, the woman beneath. What's making you so vicious?' he said in quiet disapproval.

'Bitterness,' she rasped. I hate myself! she thought helplessly. What's happening to me? What's he doing to me?

'It'll ruin you,' he said shortly. 'Take it from one who knows. Feel it by all means, then put it aside and get on with your life. I don't like——'

Tanya let her eyes harden. 'Good,' she said miserably, wanting to be the exact opposite of anything he liked. 'Suits me. You want to know what's changed me? In a nutshell, you!' The words began to flow again; everything she'd felt and thought over the years and had been ashamed to admit. 'I can't bear the way I feel, I wish I could change, but you've soured my life and *made* me bitter!' she cried jerkily.

'Then tell me how,' he breathed, his face hard, his body tense.

Her chin lifted high. 'I became bitter when Mother died. She was distraught when you vanished. I don't need to point out the connection with you and her death again, do I?'

'She knew where I'd gone,' he said gently.

Tanya rounded her eyes in outraged disbelief. 'What?'

'She knew,' he repeated firmly. 'And you must be careful about jumping to conclusions as far as her death was concerned. You see, Tanya, she was dying when I left her.'

His compassionate expression at her stunned reaction hit her with a knee-weakening force, making it hard for her to collect her thoughts. 'No!' she wailed. 'If that were true, it means she told you—but not us...!' Her voice trailed into nothing. A nagging thought had struck her. If true, this would be another secret he alone had shared. Tanya felt deeply hurt that her mother might have put her trust only in him.

'Ester didn't want to burden any of you with her illness till it was impossible to hide it any longer. At the time I left, she was dying of cancer and it was too late for surgery,' he continued relentlessly. 'Now you must realise that I couldn't have known the cause of death unless she'd told me before I left. I never saw her again, did I?'

'Lisa could have told you——' she said, desperate to prove him wrong.

'No,' he said quietly, and something in his eyes convinced her.

Tanya pressed a hand hard against her cheek to ease the pain there. 'Father didn't know till almost the last week—none of us did! Why on earth would she confide in *you*?' she croaked.

'To persuade me to stay.'

Her breath rasped in sharply. 'Oh, God!' she groaned. 'You... knew and... still you left?'

'I had to go. Now will you believe I'm not your brother?' he asked softly. He looked white, the sharp ridge of his high Slav cheekbones standing out beneath the dark hollows of his eyes. 'She wanted me to stay and pretend that I was her son. I refused.'

Confused, she walked to the window to think; her world, the past she'd known was frightening her in the way it was slipping and sliding in all directions. Things she'd thought to be true weren't true. She gripped the white silk drape tightly then turned, her eyes wary beneath her wet lashes, and she realised she'd shed tears.

'I became so bitter when Mother died,' she said in a distant voice. 'Father lost all interest in life and abandoned everything he'd worked for... all the things he'd believed in, like forgiveness and love for others. He had no emotional energy left and lost his concern for other people. It made him bitter too.' And his hatred for István, who they all thought had hastened her mother's death, had been frightening to see.

'I'm so sorry,' István said quietly. 'Lisa said you look after him now.'

'He's no trouble, and besides, we can't afford help.' Tanya spoke without resentment though the tiredness came through in her voice. 'Mariann and Sue work in London and send what they can. Mrs Lane—the new vicar's wife, who lives in the new vicarage—is looking after Father while I'm away.'

'It's a huge mausoleum of a house,' commented István. 'Too big for you to cope with alone, I'd have thought.'

'I can manage. I've learnt to run my business and the house by tight organisation,' she said curtly. 'If I've lost my malleability and gentleness, well, it's not surprising. It takes drive and grit and initiative——' She stopped in embarrassment, seeing that he was watching her curiously.

'Go on. I am interested. In your business. Let me guess. A riding school?' he hazarded.

'No,' she said shortly. 'Riding holidays. I thought you and Lisa had done a lot of talking? You know remarkably little about us.' And she could have bitten her tongue out. Of course they hadn't been discussing life in Widecombe!

He smiled faintly. 'We didn't have the time. Are these riding holidays on Dartmoor?' he asked.

'No,' she said proudly, keen to show him that she'd triumphed in difficult circumstances. No wonder she wasn't the same person he'd known. 'I set the whole thing up on the small business scheme. I sell holidays that I've packaged myself—riding in the Camargue and gypsy-caravan tours in France.'

There was nothing in his face to indicate that he was impressed with her venture or thought it small-time and doomed to failure. 'It's a bad time for the holiday business, I hear,' he remarked casually.

'I'm hanging in there. And John's arranging——' Her mouth clamped shut. 'I'm not telling you any more of my business,' she snapped.

'It's always a good idea to keep your intentions secret,' he agreed laconically.

The hint of a smile tugging again at the corner of his cynical mouth, he reached out, idly sifting through the clothes in her case before she could stop him. When he raised a pair of minute briefs high into the air and arched an incredulous eyebrow at her, it was all she could do to hold back her temper. Her blushes, however, were less controllable.

'These are *yours*?' he asked in mock-amazement. 'Daughter of a vicar——!'

'Put them down!' she demanded indignantly.

'You know,' he said, twirling the ruffled white scrap mesmerically with one practised finger, 'any stranger walking in now, seeing us in your bedroom and me rummaging in your unmentionables, would imagine that you and I——'

'Ohhh! Don't even say it!' she rasped.

'Why?' he rapped.

'Because, because—it's—it's...'

'Too momentous even to consider,' he supplied huskily.

'No!' she yelled, blocking it out stubbornly. There were things to do. Marriages to protect. Ex-lovers of the bride to be ejected! 'Just leave it alone! All I want to do is to stop you from hurting John or Lisa——'

'You'd go to the ends of the earth for the people you love, wouldn't you?' he mused, dropping her briefs into the case again. He took her by the arms, his hands sliding up and down in a maddeningly disturbing way and she was rooted to the spot in dread. Suddenly she didn't feel sisterly at all towards him and that fact added to her panic. 'Your loyalty is a trait I can make good use of,' he said silkily. 'I imagine you'll be more than willing to beg me for a favour.'

'A—a favour? What kind of favour?' she asked suspiciously.

'Any favour, I hope, to stop me ruining Lisa's wedding,' he answered smugly, strolling nonchalantly to the door.

His words slammed into her stomach with a force that shook her. 'Wait!' she gasped. 'Don't go!'

He looked at her wickedly over his shoulder. 'Begging?'

'No! But——'

'You'll regret that incredible pride,' he drawled. 'I'm going to break it.'

The door shut before she could say another word.

Damn! she cursed uncharacteristically, wrenching open the door. 'Come back here!' she demanded, her heart beating furiously.

'Is there any point, while you're so intransigent?'

'I—I'm not. I have something to ask you,' she muttered sulkily.

With arrogant self-congratulation in every line of his body, he complied, shutting the door behind him and leaning against it. 'It's taken less time than I expected. I've been waiting quite a while for this moment,' he husked. 'You and I are going to enjoy ourselves, Tanya. Just the two of us.'

'I don't know what you mean,' she grated.

'Don't you?'

The sexual implication, the invitation was plain enough. She whisked her damp palms down her hips, immobilised by her leaden body. And she knew then that he couldn't be her brother.

'No!' The word cracked into pieces. Fighting for comprehension, she moistened her dry lips, swallowed, pushed down the horror. Breathe. Slowly, steadily. She tried again. 'You're trying to—to...'

Her voice thickened and died away, unable this time to beat the choking lump in her throat. In frustration she lunged at him and flailed furiously with her fists, raining blows on his face and body, not caring where they landed——

Till he caught each fiercely clenched hand. 'I think I'm succeeding. You need proof?' he asked softly.

And he kissed her. Properly—no; more than that, he kissed her as she'd always dreamed of being kissed, one man, one woman and *fire*, their lips flaming and flowering as though they'd been made for that single purpose, that one moment, her whole life, her whole being seemingly centred on their two mouths warm and tender, gentle yet fierce.

Deep in the drugging delight of his arms, she moaned, struggling against the rising of her own frightening desire. She loathed him. No man could compare with him in his cold, calculating...

His lips moved softly, murmuring over hers, and she felt the despair of wanting something that she couldn't, shouldn't, mustn't have. He was evil, conniving. She couldn't want him—that would be too humiliating.

But he held her a prisoner and the pleasure was undeniable, the temptation almost too much to bear. István was deepening the kiss, driving his mouth against hers with a passion that reached deep inside her and awoke every slumbering cell of sexual desire in her body.

This was how it should be done. A lover's mouth should feel like this, infinitely welcome, smooth as silk, warm as the sun... Tanya gave a small whimper of protest as the pressure was lifted from her trembling lips which pouted disgracefully with lush abandon. And a hunger for more.

'I hope you're not convinced,' he whispered huskily. 'I'm perfectly prepared to give you more proof.'

Her eyes shimmered with pain. More proof. More kissing. Wonderful. Weakly she warded him off with her hands, twisting her head from his searching mouth so that his kiss landed harmlessly on her throat. Harmlessly? She gasped. Even that branding of his lips made her pulses leap and at last she was forced to acknowledge that the heat she'd felt earlier, scourging her innocent body, had been pure sexual reaction. Her body had known this, some time before her brain had reached that conclusion too.

'Stop it, stop it!' she croaked hoarsely. 'I—I accept you're not my brother!'

'Ah. I thought I was proving something else,' he complained into her tumbling, burnished hair.

The warmth of his breath shivered across her scalp. She gritted her teeth in case the shudder of delight that curled inside her body should reveal her feelings. With a determined pressure on her chin, he brought her small face around and his lips possessed hers again; he possessed *her* with a totality that weakened her resolve.

Helplessly she found herself floating in a dream world, every bit as much of a stupid, unreal fantasy as the years

they'd spent together as brother and sister. And now...
She moaned and struggled in his arms, appalled that he
seemed determined to make their relationship even more
intimate than before.

CHAPTER THREE

THE shock, the certainty of what Tanya had half feared to be true, was too much to bear. And the explosive release of her feelings petrified her. She wanted to throw caution, wisdom and restraint to the winds. Somewhere buried in her hatred for István there seemed to be a wanton desire to surrender to the unfair pleasure of his calculated onslaught.

His kisses rained on her lips, tracing their swollen lines with special, deliciously detailed attention to the corners... 'Ohhh!' She shuddered helplessly.

'We're getting somewhere,' he muttered thickly. 'The removal of the first veil. Seduction should always be slow and enjoyed to the full, don't you think?'

She hardly registered what he'd said. Despite all sense, she'd abandoned her lips to him. 'Oh, oh, ohhh!' she groaned, appalled to discover how far he'd gone and what he was doing to her mortifyingly willing body. Her jacket was open. His hands were on her shirt, teasing through the soft fabric and shaping with tender, cradling movements the fullness of her breasts. 'István!' she protested weakly.

'Easy,' he husked, misunderstanding her agonised cries. Or, she wondered desperately, did he perhaps understand them better than she? 'We have plenty of time.'

'Time?' she mumbled, and threw her head back in an agonised delight at the new sensations flowing through her too eager body. He was hurtling her towards disaster and she was willing him on! How could she? 'István!' she whispered, not wanting the caress ever to end.

Each breast tautened beneath his expert, subtle touch. The soft material that must be her jacket briefly fell

50

against the back of her ankles. She knew she should deny him the liberties he was already taking. But the lines between her brain and her mouth seemed to be engaged; her hands were wonderfully occupied in feeling the latent power of his biceps as his fingers flipped her buttons undone; her loins were... Oh, no, no, no! She groaned, recognising with shame that her whole hungry body was conspiring against her.

Tantalisingly slow in his movements, he opened her shirt and she watched his reaction to her body as though her life depended on it. Somewhere in the depths of her mind she registered the fact that she wanted him to find her beautiful and to admire her deeply tanned body. Without realising it, she lifted her ribcage in the age-old gesture of woman to man, riveted to the glow of his black eyes. Her breathing ceased while she waited for his response.

The quiver of shock that rippled through his body made her quiver with deep, feminine delight. He muttered something thickly in Hungarian then, 'Oh, Tanya!' he husked, looking, just looking.

She was flattered. Heaven help her, she rejoiced that he admired what he saw. Touch me, touch me! her nerves screamed. 'Stop this!' she said thickly.

'I can't. Oh, Tanya!' he growled, his mouth sultry with desire. And when she was about to reward her taut body by reaching out for his hand, he slid warm palms to the eager thrust of her breasts.

'You mustn't——!' Dry lips. Slick them. Deny him. Break the spell! Why, oh, why wouldn't her mind connect with her body? She knew she was behaving as if she had no morals. He shouldn't be doing this... 'Uhhh!' She quivered.

The pressure of his thumbs, flicking over each nipple, had rocked her on her feet. The tender kiss that accompanied it trembled on her mouth as though he felt touched by her helplessness. Or was that a smile?

'Hell!' he muttered shakily.

Fool. Where were her wits, her voice? 'No. No,' she mumbled unconvincingly.

'Too late to play games,' he growled softly.

'I'm not playing a game!' she croaked.

'Neither am I.'

Grim. Determined. 'We can't——!'

'Sure we can. Nothing to stop us,' he breathed.

She lost her balance—or, rather, he toppled her over deliberately so that the soft duvet on the bed puffed around them like an embrace when they fell on to it. Snuggled down in the conspiringly cosy warmth, her breath and his loud and harsh, she watched wide-eyed and frightened as he leaned menacingly over her, his intent absolutely clear as he slowly slid his hands up the smoothness of her thighs.

'*No!*' she gasped, rolling away frantically. She stood up on shaky legs and scanned the room desperately for her shirt. It had been flung far across the room, an action she hadn't even registered. Her shaky hand flew to her brow in bewilderment.

István lay back on the bed, his hands behind the gleaming cap of his dark hair, an action that managed to force her heart into her throat. 'Try running for it,' he challenged huskily.

The piercing flame of his eyes on her taut, voluptuous breasts caused them to glow and prickle with heat. Run? Judging by the carnal look on his face, he meant to catch her, tumble with her to the ground and enjoy every moment. To say nothing of enjoying the movement of her body as she scurried across the bedroom floor.

Too late, she realised that she was being brazen in not covering herself up and folded her arms defensively across her chest, blushing furiously. 'You bastard!' she cried wildly.

His lashes flickered and she remembered uncomfortably that her taunt was probably true. 'Go for it,' was all he said.

Her eyes wary, she walked as haughtily as she could to where her shirt lay and tried to turn it the right side out. Failing. 'Darn!' she muttered in frustration.

Long arms reached around her. She went rigid at the feel of his body against her naked back but, short of tearing the shirt, she had to surrender it and let him calmly organise it and feed the sleeves up her arms, across her back, and swing her around with every intention—she'd imagined innocently—of doing it up.

Instead, he grunted deep in his throat and bent his dark head. Which she cradled in her hands, groaning with the sudden ferocious passion she felt as his mouth closed on one nipple and suckled hungrily.

'István!' She shuddered in pure, astonished ecstasy.

'I know,' he muttered hoarsely, moving to the other breast.

She felt her inhibitions slipping away. Her body had a life of its own, an alarming life, riddled with lust, and every inch of her was crying out for his touch, his mouth, the release that his dark eyes promised. A moan whispered from her bruised lips as she realised that she couldn't resist the urges of her body any more, that István's fingers, his lips, his tongue were arousing her beyond all sanity.

There was a look of bliss on his face that half broke her heart. I want this, she thought helplessly. I want him. How could I ever have blamed Lisa for being seduced by him?

And a more earth-shattering conclusion came to her too. How could she blame István for surrendering to the same uncontrollable passion she was now feeling? Only now did she know what it was like to want something—someone—beyond all sanity. It was the first time she'd ever understood the power of passion.

Lisa, she reminded herself. His true purpose was to seduce *Lisa*. He was only using her. Appalled, she searched for something to stop him—to stop herself. And found it.

'István! Don't go any further! Is it your intention,' she grated harshly, 'to get *me* pregnant too?'

His look of pleasure was wiped clean away. For a moment, his mouth remained closed over the hard peak of her heavy breast, his tongue still poised in a warm, moist curl beneath. Then all contact with her was abruptly withdrawn and when he rose his eyes were like hard black stones.

'Oh, Tanya. You *have* changed,' he said in a viciously soft growl. 'Quite the little bitch.'

Deeply unhappy with the way she'd behaved, she hastily drew the shirt edges together and fumbled with the buttons that seemed to be conspiring with him in their refusal to meet.

'Only because you're such a brute!' she cried miserably. 'I know what you're doing, you see!'

'Do you? I suppose that makes it easier for me,' he drawled, but his voice was jerky as though his control was wavering. 'Shall we compare notes? Tell me what I'm up to.'

'No good!' she seethed, almost hysterical with humiliation. 'You were making a point, weren't you?'

'I suppose I was,' he said slowly.

She winced. 'Point taken,' she said tightly. 'I can see you're more dangerous than I thought. If you can briefly overcome someone who actually hates you——'

'Briefly overcome?' he queried, his eyes glinting with dangerous lights. His finger lightly brushed one nipple, then the other. Leaving her quivering. Melting. Furious. 'Be honest,' he murmured. 'The atmosphere around us has been steaming ever since you suspected we weren't brother and sister.'

Her tongue slicked over her dry lips. She'd murder him, she thought hysterically, glaring at his self-satisfied face. What he needed was something to wipe that smile *off*.

'Because I was angry!' she said defiantly. 'You moved in on me when I was reeling from learning something I should have guessed ages ago. You've been a cuckoo in the nest all these years. I was shocked and you thought you'd take advantage—but you're not that clever, István! The moment I could think straight, I knew that you were kissing me to prove how irresistible you were and then——'

'Then what?' he growled. A black brow winged up. 'OK, you're so telepathic, read my mind.'

'It's not difficult since it's one-track!' she wailed. 'I know perfectly well that you were going to move on to Lisa!'

He tensed, his expression like stone. 'I was? On the eve of her wedding?' he asked tightly.

'You're capable of anything!' she retorted angrily. 'You intended to worm your way into her room——'

'The bridal suite,' he reminded her through clenched teeth. 'The same suite where she and John are staying for a few days when the guests leave.'

'Wouldn't that give your jaded palate a kick?' she muttered, wishing she hadn't gone quite so far.

His jaw was rigid. 'Do you really think that I could seduce Lisa there, knowing that will be their marriage bed?'

Louder and louder, her heart pounded in her ears. Tanya stared at the hard-eyed stranger with the ruthless, cruel mouth and tried to equate him with the person who'd once shown occasional kindness to her when she was a child. A rage was racking his body, bunching the muscles, increasing in violence the longer she hesitated.

She thought of the door, smashed by István in ice-cold fury when her father had grounded him for a weekend. The shocked silence after he'd bloodied his playground tormenters for calling him 'gypsy'. And...

'I remember those three days before you left,' she said in a shaky whisper. 'You'd quarrelled with Mother. You wouldn't speak or eat. You sat at the table as if you were made of ice and Mother howled and pleaded with you and it made no difference at all. You refused to respond. You were indifferent to her distress even though you knew then that she had only a short time to live. Yes. I think you are capable of anything.'

A vast breath lifted his ribcage and was slowly released in an obvious effort to gain control of the storm that gripped his body. 'God give me strength!' A huge breath shuddered in and out of his barrel chest. 'Tanya,' he said hoarsely, in something strangely like a plea.

'No! I won't be swayed by you! Let's stick to what really worries me,' she said shakily, refusing to acknowledge the lurch of her treacherous, compassionate heart. 'You mean to ruin John's happiness. You always resented Father's love for him; you always tried to make John look a fool beside you.'

'John tried to be me,' he said curtly. 'For that, he *was* a fool. He had qualities of his own and didn't need to ape mine. He should never have tried to climb the crags that I did when he had no head for heights. He should never have tried to tame the wild ponies on the moors as I did, either. No wonder he got injured time and time again; no wonder Lisa spent half her time mopping blood off him——'

'You made him look less than a man,' Tanya complained bitterly.

'He did that on his own without any help from me! He was determined to play on my pitch,' István said irritably, 'instead of finding one of his own. God in heaven! No one in their right mind would have changed places with me!'

'Wouldn't they? The favourite son? Idolised by every female he met? The envy of every male? With good looks, brains, physical skills and as much money as he could ever want?' she derided. There was surprise on his face and she groaned inwardly that she'd been rash enough to reveal her own feelings by describing him so favourably in the heat of the moment.

'Did I look happy?' was all he said, however.

Pained, she averted her gaze from his. Not often. Not even now. Why had she glimpsed sadness whenever he'd thought no one was looking at him? There had been a remote melancholy, a yearning for something distant and unreachable, the hint of a secret demon that had plagued him. Long ago she'd imagined that her unquestioning, undemanding devotion had somehow gentled the wildness in him and that had given her comfort. No, he hadn't been happy, but she was mystified why that should have been the case.

'You're manipulating me,' she said slowly. 'Trying to appeal to my emotions.'

'Of course. Though things are going more slowly than I'd planned because you're so darn stubborn.'

The mockery had returned. Infuriated that she'd nearly been taken in, she let her eyes blaze with anger. 'I won't let you treat me like a pawn in your life! And I'm going to protect Lisa from you too so that she doesn't fall straight into your arms!'

'Hush,' he murmured. 'She's next door. She'll hear you.'

'I don't care!' Tanya succeeded at last in fastening the final few buttons and scurried for her jacket. Something had to disguise her body's horrifying need for him. That medieval armour might do the trick, she thought gloomily, bending down and scooping up the heap of linen. Straightening proudly, she said, 'I'm telling Lisa what you've tried to do. She's got to know about your——'

'Why don't you wear a bra?' he enquired idly.

'Ohhh!' Mad as a hornet, she flung the telephone at him. 'Get out!' she screamed, relieved that he'd ducked out of danger.

'Such a high level of secret abandon is rather surprising,' he commented thoughtfully. 'I shall think of it and wonder about its implications all through dinner.'

'Dinner? You're staying to the party?' she asked in dismay.

'Of course. Lisa gave me an invitation. I'm going to get my money's worth. In the meantime, can you solve the puzzle of a woman who wears "Keep Off" signs and yet is semi-nude beneath?'

Despite the sultry tone, he was in total control of himself again—and she knew that she must be so if she were to handle this situation. Frowning, she sought an explanation other than the real one: that she loved the feel of sensual materials against her body, that, whatever her exterior severity, inside she revelled in the fact that silk or satin was touching her flesh.

'You work it out,' she muttered.

'I have. The answer's hedonism,' he said quietly. 'The clues have always been there. Like…stroking your pony's mane and nuzzling into it, rubbing your cheek against my puppy's soft coat, rolling half-nude in the meadow till you were covered in pollen and the scent of wild flowers.'

She flushed, embarrassed. 'I was wearing a bathing costume!' she muttered. 'And I was only thirteen.'

Thirteen. Too young to know why she loved to lie in the field and feel the clover and smooth grass-blades against her bare skin. Too young, even at fourteen, to know why she had hugged his back so hard when he'd taken her on the back of his motorbike for the very first time, and why the thrill of the ride had been rivalled by the warm softness of the leather and the hard masculinity of his beautiful back.

Hedonist. Was she? That was worrying.

'Cooee!'

Tanya started violently at the sound of Lisa's voice outside, the relief palpable in her pale face.

'Lisa would never make a comedienne. Her timing's too bad,' said István laconically. 'Come in, Lisa, if you must!' he called and shook his head at Tanya with a sigh of regret as if he had unfinished business.

The door was hesitantly pushed open. 'Oh.' Lisa looked anxiously from one to the other and her voice was tremulous when she spoke again. 'What—what have you two been up to?' she asked with a wavering cheerfulness.

'Grappling,' Tanya said bitterly. 'Nothing unusual about that.'

'Do *you* wear a bra?' István asked Lisa earnestly.

'Shut up!' Tanya yelled.

Her face the colour of a Turner sunset at its height, she gritted her teeth at his implication: Tanya doesn't; is that true of you too? Lisa's jaw had dropped open as if she could hardly believe what she'd heard.

'For heaven's sake, you lot,' complained John, appearing suddenly in the doorway behind Lisa. 'Get a move on! The party's about to start——'

'I thought it had,' drawled István, slanting a wicked glance at Tanya. 'We were well away, up here, for a moment or two——'

'You were about to get sent off for foul play,' she snapped.

'She's having a bit of an identity crisis,' he explained to the others.

'Patronise me any more,' she said tightly, 'and you'll be having an identity crisis yourself, because I'll have separated your brain from your body.' Uncomfortably aware of the shocked silence, she passed a tired hand over her forehead but felt determined not to apologise. 'I'm a bit shattered from getting up so early,' she said stiffly. 'I need to wash and change.'

'I'll stay and chat, big-brother style, while you do,' he offered genially.

She turned an icy glare on the butter-mouthed István. 'Why don't you drop dead?' she snapped, so miserable that she hardly knew what she was saying. Everyone stared and she went scarlet with shame.

'Too many things to do first.' István met her gaze levelly. 'Be warned. I don't fight fire with fire. I fight it with oxy-acetylene burners, and any opposition with a battering-ram.' Tanya shivered at his softly menacing growl, more afraid of him than she'd ever been. Her huge slanting eyes were transfixed by his unblinking gaze. '*Think*,' he said grimly. 'Stop accepting without question everything you're told and put that brain of yours to work. I'll be downstairs. I expect you'll want to talk to me later, ask me questions.'

Tanya's brows met over her nose. She was consumed with curiosity. Mysteries were for solving and she ached to know how, why, who, when... Oh, all the questions in the world were beginning to form in her mind now that he wasn't distracting her with his sinful mouth. But his vanity would be flattered if she asked about his background. It would seem as though she was interested, even as though she cared, and that was the last thing she wanted.

Catch-22. Why did he always put her in impossible situations?

'I'm not asking you any questions,' she said haughtily; 'I don't give a toss who——'

'Don't say any more!' he ordered quickly. 'This is between us so keep it that way.'

'There's nothing between us,' she retorted vehemently. 'I don't even know why I ever passed the time of day with you.'

'Stick around and I'll strip off enough veils for you to work out the answer to that one,' he said grimly. 'But in the meantime, what I told you is not to be broadcast around.'

'I would have thought that every member of my family has a right to know,' she began heatedly.

'Not so. Only you,' he said softly.

'Why only me?' she demanded.

István's black eyes glittered with mockery. 'You've been stubborn and blind all your life. I knew that this would be something you'd have to work out for yourself, slowly and painfully. At the moment you'd never believe the truth if I told you and decorated it with horse brasses.'

'I wasn't aware you were on nodding terms with truth,' she said waspishly. They all stared at her in astonishment and she felt upset. 'He makes me mad!' she yelled, trying to explain her sudden surprise launch into bitchiness. And where John looked bewildered, Lisa was apparently trying not to smile. István, she noticed, had returned to his more normally deadpan, unreadable self.

'I think you need time to go over the emotions you've been experiencing,' he said quietly. 'Think about the things I've told you, the inconsistencies. But I warn you, Tanya, if you so much as breathe a word of what I've told you, I'll cause trouble the like of which you've never known in your life before. And you know I can do that, don't you?'

The silence when he left was deafening. Trembling from the effects of everything that had happened since she'd set foot on Hungarian soil, she stared at the panelled door vacantly, trying to gather her wits together.

'What's going on between you two?' frowned John.

'Nothing!' she muttered.

'Tanya...' Lisa bit her lip. 'Don't be cross. He's—he's more bark than bite——'

She rounded on her friend, astonished she'd taken that tack. 'Don't defend him!' she cried unhappily. 'How can you? After what he——' Just in time, she checked herself, deeply distressed that she'd almost reminded Lisa of the pregnancy. A wave of nausea washed over her because she'd almost revealed Lisa's secret to John. He didn't even know that Lisa had lost István's baby. What price their marriage if he did? 'Oh, Lisa, look what he's doing to us! He's even got us quarrelling now,' she said bitterly.

'Give him a chance,' pleaded Lisa. 'Spend some time with him and——'

'You must be joking! I can't stand being anywhere near him,' she rasped irritably.

'Please! He's been seriously misunderstood!' protested Lisa.

John swore viciously and stomped out leaving the door swinging violently on its hinges. Tanya stared wide-eyed after her brother, her body chilled with the knowledge that István's evil influence had begun to take effect on their lives, souring what should be happy family hours ahead.

'Oh, you fool! You're acting like an absolute idiot!' she said fiercely to Lisa. 'Defend István again like that

and you risk losing a decent, loving husband! You know
how those two hate each other! You can't possibly take
István's side without causing a great deal of hurt to the
man you love. István is trouble! He'll smash your marriage just for kicks because he can't bear anyone else
being happy!'

'You're wrong!' husked Lisa. 'He's——'

'Don't! I can't bear to hear you making excuses for
him!' wailed Tanya. She threw her head back in despair
and gave an agonised groan. Lisa seemed determined to
speak well of István. It was quite inexplicable and made
her edgier, more worried than ever.

'He's been good to me——'

'Has he? Then it's because he wants something! Oh,
give me strength!' she groaned, seeing Lisa's sullen expression. There was only one thing for it. A stiff re-
minder. She had to be cruel to be kind. 'Lisa, love, have
you completely forgotten what he did to you?' she asked
huskily, knowing she would hurt her friend by referring
to the past. Yet how else could she force some sense into
that lovely blonde head?

'No,' sighed Lisa, her blue eyes troubled. She caught
Tanya's hands in hers. 'It's because I remember what he
did that I'm ... I'm begging you to understand that I
can't hate him just because you think I should——'

'You love him!' whispered Tanya, aghast.

'Yes—no—I mean——' stumbled Lisa miserably.

'Don't tell me!' Tanya groaned. 'I don't think I want
to hear any more.' She swallowed, preparing for the
awful truth. 'Your marriage to John——'

'That's not in question,' said Lisa unhappily. 'Of
course I'm marrying him.'

Tanya bit hard into her lower lip. Marriage without
love? Or did she love John and it was only István's dazzling presence, his wicked, persuasive eyes, that was
swaying Lisa from the straight and narrow? She must
do everything possible to heal this breach, she
thought miserably.

'Listen!' she said urgently. 'István's driving a wedge between us—intentionally or otherwise. I can't let that go on. We're both edgy and he knows it. You're on the eve of your wedding, I'm...overwrought.'

'Why?' probed Lisa, with a sharp look.

She pushed a smile out, mechanically lifting the corners of her mouth and decided on being economical with the truth. There was no point in worrying her friend about István's revelations—or the attempted seduction.

'Trouble with the business, you know. I'm rather worried.'

'Oh, Tan! I'm sorry,' Lisa sighed.

'It'll be OK, I'm sure. All's not lost. I've got terrific prospects here, thanks to John,' Tanya confided. 'He's worked behind the scenes to give me a chance of getting the sole rights for a package deal with a Lippizaner riding school. Keep it under your hat—I don't want anyone else getting the same idea. Let's get some time with one another and we'll feel like our old selves,' she suggested, attempting to be cheerful and positive. It would make sense if she kept Lisa strictly under her eye, too. 'Can't have the bride being upset, can we—or her bridesmaid? Sue and Mariann will be here soon. Don't let them get pulled into this awful wrangle that István's engineered. Please.'

She and Lisa reflected the misery in each other's eyes. Tanya thought of the bond that had held them inseparable since they were first wheeled in their prams to the old yew tree in the village square and their mothers had sat on the old wooden seat and chatted companionably.

Their friendship had been the last thing that István hadn't destroyed up to now. Yet, inexplicably, he was attacking that too. Hating to be close to anyone himself, he seemed envious of the warmth that existed between others. So he maliciously set out to destroy it. No one could respect a guy who was that petty. Something inside her mourned the man she'd *thought* he was.

'I love you, Lisa,' she said quietly. 'You've always been like one of my sisters. Closer, perhaps: they had each other; I had you. We've shared so much together, come through so much pain. Don't let anything change that!'

Lisa's arms came around her securely. 'Course not, Tan,' she sniffed. 'I'm not surprised you're edgy. Let's take five.'

'I think I need fifty,' smiled Tanya ruefully.

'Fifty will do! Put on that white dress you wrote to me about and knock us all silly.' They exchanged watery, sniffy smiles. 'This'll be a night to remember, I promise,' said Lisa, sounding more positive. 'Let's have fun!'

'Sure.' Tanya brushed back a tear and managed a husky laugh. 'We'll show the Magyars how Devon girls can party!'

Lisa's eyes shone. 'And... keep your peace with István,' she begged. 'Try to see his side of things, whatever he does, whatever he says. I—I know you don't want to talk about him, but... oh, Tan, he means a lot to me.'

'Lisa——' she began in anxious warning.

'No. Hear me out. He once did something totally un-selfish that he knew would reflect badly on his character.'

'What?' she asked disbelievingly.

Lisa hung her head. 'I can't say. It's for him to tell you.'

A secret. She and István had a secret. Tanya frowned. 'I doubt it was truly unselfish. He would have had reasons of his own for doing it, whatever it was. And it would be no skin off his nose, anyway. Nothing could make his reputation any worse than it was,' Tanya muttered, alarmed at the tears in Lisa's eyes. 'Oh, you fool! I do believe you've still got a crush on him,' she sighed.

'I admire him,' Lisa answered stubbornly. 'And I'm asking you this huge favour: don't ruffle the water to-night. It would mean so much to me if you and he didn't quarrel. Hold your peace. Swear?'

Peace! When she wanted to tie a rope around his neck and string him from the highest tree! 'Nothing's going to spoil this lovely evening,' she promised, evading the real issue.

But later, when Lisa had gone, she sat down on the bed and found that she was incapable of doing anything, let alone unpacking. Too much was whirling around in her mind. Lisa carried a torch for István still, despite the fact he'd seduced her with no thought for the consequences.

Tanya thought back to the dramatic come-at-once phone call she'd had from Lisa four years ago. And the discovery when she arrived at her house that her beloved friend was writhing on her bed in fear and pain. Lisa's hysterical scream rang in her ears again...

'I'm losing my child! Your brother's child!'

Tanya clenched her fists till her nails dug into her palms. It had been terrible, witnessing Lisa's anguish, and for Tanya it had been the final nail in the coffin as far as her affection towards István was concerned. Any remaining respect had been wiped away.

It was she who'd called the ambulance and Lisa's elderly parents—now dead. It was she who'd summoned István, and after speaking privately to Lisa he'd relayed her wishes that no one should know what had happened. So it was generally believed that Lisa was in hospital for 'female trouble'. John had never known a thing.

It still had the power to sicken her to the stomach. Lisa's parents had pressured István to leave the area. She herself had added to that pressure by seeking him out and screaming abuse at him, driven to extremes perhaps by her own sense of deep disappointment that he was flawed. He'd behaved badly, in a flagrantly irresponsible way. Lisa was young and naïve and he'd callously taken advantage of her.

At the time, Tanya had been afraid that her father's position as vicar of the parish would be untenable if the news ever became common knowledge. The irony was

that it wouldn't have mattered. István wasn't a real
member of her family at all! So...who was he?

She wandered around the room restlessly, engrossed
in doing what István had suggested: thinking things
through. He must be Hungarian; all the signs pointed
to that. Could he be part of her mother's unspoken past?
Everyone had imagined that her mother had suffered as
a refugee from Communist rule and her wish never to
discuss her homeland had been respected.

Yet it didn't make sense. Apparently her mother had
taken charge of a Hungarian woman's child and passed
him off as her own. Why? Since her mother must have
arrived in England with the child, Tanya realised that
her father had been party to the deception. The most
extraordinary thing was that her parents hadn't told them
the truth years ago.

She wondered when István had known and if that was
why he'd always been so distant. But however much she
racked her brains she still couldn't explain why so much
money had been spent on István's education and general
upbringing.

She leaned against the bedpost, her mind empty and
incapable of untangling the mess. She was too
overwhelmed with the events and the strain of the last
hour or so to shuffle her brain cells into order. Later,
she promised herself wearily. One thing at a time.

As for the kiss... Embarrassment painted her face
with a soft pink and she thought wryly that she'd never
blushed so much in all her life. But then she'd never
come face to face with the fact that she'd lived in great
intimacy with someone who wasn't even related to her.

Scowling, refusing to examine why she felt alarmingly
excited that there was no blood link at all with István,
she mechanically sorted out her clothes and punished
herself with a quick, chilly bath instead of her usual glorious soak.

With rapid and efficient movements, she pulled on
her long, narrow-skirted dress that skimmed her body
so beguilingly. She smiled wryly as she adjusted the

narrow straps. The dress was a wow! She blessed Sue for making it so beautifully. The thin white cotton flattered her golden skin, the two slits up the side quite modest till she moved and then——

'Oh, you fool,' she groaned under her breath. 'He'll think you're deliberately egging him on!'

Her hands smoothed down the slight curve of her hips and she practised walking decorously, her eyes anxiously fixed to the mirror. However small her steps, there seemed to be an endless shimmer of gleaming bare leg and thigh on view.

He'd mocked one of her dresses before; the one she'd worn for her first dance. A 'come-and-get-me dress', he'd called it, and had ordered her in clipped, angry tones to put on something befitting the daughter of a vicar. So she'd ended up in the flowery print with the Peter Pan collar and hadn't been asked to dance all night. István had actually sounded pleased about that when he'd picked her up later! He'd enjoyed spoiling her fun!

This time, she thought grimly, her eyes gleaming rebelliously, she'd darn well wear what she chose, would 'wow' whoever she wanted and have a really good time to make up for that awful début. After all, her two sisters would be dressed to kill!

And instead of sleeking her hair back into a 'Miss Prim' chignon as she'd planned, she scooped up the shiny, slippery chestnut curtain in a casual style and let strands of it escape as though she'd been tumbling in the hay.

It looked remarkably sexy. She'd never thought of herself in that way before. Experimenting, she eased out a deep wave of shimmering hair so that it drifted seductively over one eye. Her self-conscious giggle was interrupted by a knock on the door.

'Come in, Lisa, darling!' she cried, deciding to get a giggle out of her friend too. Cement the bond between them. Lisa would laugh like crazy! 'Get a load of *this*——!'

Her mock-sexy imitation of Madonna in full shimmy was frozen in mid-execution by the sight of a sultry-mouthed István. He hungrily surveyed her provocative pose and the raw desire in his eyes began to create chaos inside her body again.

'I'm getting it,' he drawled slowly. 'I'm getting it in every cell of my body. The load is a little hard to bear.'

'I—I——'

She stared back, rooted to the spot by his appearance. Men didn't wear dinner-jackets in Devon much, especially in remote villages on Dartmoor. Life there revolved around the local fairs, casual barn dances and jeans-and-jumper parties. This elegant, dazzling István was something of a shock. Dumb with a sudden, devastating ache, she devoured him, from his glossy raven's-wing hair, the sharply tailored jacket and ruffled shirt, down to his gleaming black shoes. Her hand fluttered nervously at her breast and his eyes followed her movement avidly.

'It's getting to me a little further down than that,' he breathed.

'István!' she remonstrated hoarsely. Her too! she thought, aghast, identifying the rich glow deep in the core of her body.

'Hot in here suddenly. Sultry. Makes your loins weak, doesn't it?' he said, his satiny voice gliding through every inch of her.

How did he *know*? she thought wildly. Was he guessing? 'Not particularly,' she said, but her attempt at sounding casual failed dismally because he was contemplating the exposed length of her thigh with an intensely carnal interest as though he meant to... Hastily she drew her leg in to stand more primly. 'If you imagine for one minute that I'm wearing this because I want to attract you, then you're wrong,' she began shakily.

His hands spread in a gesture of mock-bewilderment. 'But what other explanation is there? You don't know any other available man here,' he reasoned with a

mocking arrogance. 'Am I to take it, then, that you're
just offering yourself...in general?' he added insolently.

'Certainly not!' she spluttered. 'You're the promiscuous one, not me! You're the man who got Lisa
pr——'

In two strides, he'd reached her and had caught her
wrists in a grip like an iron manacle. 'God!' he growled
savagely. 'Throw that at me again and I'll really lose my
temper! I wish I'd never——!' He cut himself off
irritably.

'Me too! I wish "you'd never"!' she cried piteously.

'Damn you for that!' he muttered through his teeth.

The hazel of her eyes turned a deep forest-green with
anguish. 'Oh, István, leave this place before it's too late!'
she cried brokenly. 'Leave Lisa alone. Leave me alone!'

'I can't,' he whispered harshly. 'There's something I
must do.'

'No!' she moaned, knowing now without a doubt that
he was determined to make love to Lisa tonight.

But he silenced her protest with his lips, jerking her
head back and grinding his mouth on hers in a frightening display of uncontrollable passion. Then she was
released.

Panting, surveying him from under her lashes and
touching her wounded mouth with trembling fingers, she
could only shudder. A whirlwind had hit her again.
István.

'Easy, isn't it?' he taunted. 'I'll do what I want, get
what I want,' he growled softly. 'I always have, always
will. And very soon. You can be sure of that.' Tanya
swallowed, her eyes on the breadth of his shoulders,
clearly defined by the well-tailored jacket. 'Enjoy the
anticipation,' he added huskily as he went through
the door.

CHAPTER FOUR

THE whole late afternoon and early evening passed in a blur. Anyone watching would have said that Tanya was having a good time. There was this white figure, dancing as furiously as the lights from the crystal chandeliers that sparkled in her glossily bouncing hair. There was this face, permanently laughing.

But when she tilted her head back to the exuberantly painted ceilings, it was to hide the blankness of her eyes, the pain that suddenly hollowed her heart and made her wince.

It should have been the party of a lifetime. John and Lisa's Hungarian friends were warm and friendly and flung themselves quite uninhibitedly into the serious business of having a good time.

Without István's unnerving presence, it could have been the fairy-tale she'd dreamed of, Tanya thought wistfully. Elegant, gilded chairs around the ballroom; greenery and ribbons bedecking the grand portraits and potted palm trees; discreet flunkeys bearing trays of a never-ending supply of champagne; happy, vital faces.

In the arms of admittedly fascinating men who were sadly wasted on her, she continued to dance, around the perfectly sprung ballroom floor, out on to the candlelit terrace, whirling between the satinwood tables in the west hall. In the mirrors there she saw herself, flushed, sinuous, head back in animated conversation, bent with romantic ardour by a dark-eyed Hungarian who moved, like all of his race, as though the music was in his blood.

But she remained as cold as Alaska inside.

Her eyes searched for István more times than she wanted to admit. Searched and found, for he seemed to be watching her closely—and still managing to dazzle every female in sight.

'Anticipating destiny?' came his mocking drawl as they glided close to one another.

Her whole body flooded with heat. 'Not at all. Having a wonderful time!' she cried, beaming stupidly at her partner.

'But oh, the den of wild things, in the darkness of her eyes!' he husked, as though quoting poetry.

Her smile wobbled then recovered. Her partner was politely allowing them to converse, believing István to be her brother. She flicked an irritated glance at her tormentor. 'Den of wild things' described *his* eyes rather well.

She quailed. 'I do believe you're drunk,' was the only retort she could come up with.

He slid a hand to her waist and she arched away from it, towards her startled and subsequently pink-faced partner. 'And the standard reply to that is that I'm intoxicated,' he said softly. 'And so are you. Makes the hormones fair race along, doesn't it?'

Laughing, he moved away with a woman in his arms who looked quite spaniel-eyed in her adoration. Tanya gritted her teeth at the sharp, slicing jealousy inside her.

Yes, she was intoxicated, fizzing with the sexual electricity he'd directed at her. How easy she was! She shuddered. If he should switch on all four bars of his electric fire for Lisa...!

'*Tan!*'

She whirled to see her sisters running down the main stairs, already in party gear. Presumably, she decided, a shaky smile of welcome spreading over her face, they'd arrived and dashed up to do a rapid change. Mariann wouldn't want to miss any partying! she thought fondly.

'My sisters are here! We see each other so rarely— Christmas, birthdays... Do excuse me!' she said smilingly to her partner in case his feelings were hurt. 'Oh, Sue! Mariann!' she cried emotionally, flinging her arms around both sisters at once.

'Good grief!' Mariann laughed, extracting herself eventually. A slender hand slicked back the short, bouncy hair behind her ears and she wriggled out of her wrap to display an eye-opening brief skirt and strapless top. 'The occasion's really got to you! Do I taste salt! This is Tan, my calm, composed sister—with tears in her eyes? You've gone all sentimental on us!'

'Catch me weeping at weddings!' grinned Sue, her slender figure dressed more decently in a honey-gold trouser suit. 'I'm not getting tied up for *years*, not till I'm financially independent. John's crazy, marrying so young!'

'Love makes you crazy,' Tanya said shakily. She mopped up her tears and kissed her sisters impetuously again. She needed family at this moment very badly.

'How right you are, Tan. Hi, girls,' murmured István, his hand lightly on Tanya's shoulder. She stiffened and he chuckled to see her sisters' open-mouthed amazement at his unexpected presence. 'The sheep has returned to the fold,' he drawled by way of explanation.

'Wolf,' corrected Tanya succinctly. 'And he's on the prowl.'

'Naughty!' he chided. 'We really must keep up family appearances, whatever the truth.'

'Why?' muttered Tanya rebelliously.

'For Lisa's sake. This is her Big Day,' he said, the platitude sounding incongruous on his cynical lips. 'Tan's a bit emotional,' he purred to her sisters.

'We noticed,' grinned Mariann, her shrewd eyes flicking from Tanya to István.

'I'm not emotional,' grated Tanya, knowing her behaviour was proving her wrong. 'Only I've had this renegade up to *here*.' Her stiffly horizontal hand indicated her chin.

'Only that far? I must do better. There is more to come,' he promised. 'When I do something, it's a head-to-toe job.'

She pretended a delicate shudder of distaste to cover up the fiercely sexual response of her treacherous hormones. They were doing more than race along. They seemed to have won the race hands down, she thought wryly.

'You sound like an undertaker,' she said acidly.

István's mouth curved into an unfairly delightful smile at her sisters' blank astonishment. 'As you see, she's not herself. Now do smile, girls, we're the centre of attention. Small wonder. Everyone's asking,' he confided, his cheek unbearably close to Tanya's, 'who *are* those three beauties with chestnut hair and almond eyes and gorgeous Hungarian cheekbones. Shall I tell them you're my sisters?' He paused, tipping his head enquiringly.

Tanya flung him a painfully sunny smile. 'Or shall you go and annoy someone else?' she suggested sweetly.

'Not bad,' he approved. 'You're hiding your feelings quite well. Just a tiny bit more of an effort...' His fingers playfully tipped up the corners of her mouth a little more. 'There!' he said in satisfaction when her breath shivered in at his touch. 'That's better.'

'Do that again,' Tanya said through her fixed grin, 'and I'll bury my stiletto heel in your foot.'

'Tut, tut,' he chided. 'What happened to the Prodigal Son? The Biblical advice to turn the other cheek?'

'Don't you quote the Bible to me!' she snapped. The strain of keeping up appearances was beginning to tell on her good nature. Her smile was slipping and so was her temper! 'He's being a real *pain*,' she muttered to her sisters. 'Don't be fooled by his smarm. I'll never forgive him, never.'

'This is Christian charity and mercy?' he wondered.

His sarcasm made Tanya wince. It went against all her upbringing to be unforgiving, but... 'Oh, you'd try the patience of a saint!' she seethed.

'Well, we make progress; the Dance of the Seven Veils gets faster, the bells are beginning to swing,' he mocked. 'Now, I'm sure you want to get rid of me with the minimum of fuss,' he went on, addressing his remarks to Sue and Mariann, 'so let's do it smoothly. I'll in-

troduce you both to a few suitably pole-axed men and
bow out disgracefully.'

And he removed the very people Tanya had wanted
around her for a while, to help restore her shattered
nerves.

'Sadist!' she muttered crossly under her breath.

He turned around as if he'd heard, his dark eyes
amused, and then he was swamped by willing dance
partners for her beautiful sisters. Suddenly she realised
that she was being inundated with offers again, and
gratefully accepted the chance to dance her feet off and
avoid thinking about István or his sinister intentions.

'Eat, drink and be merry, for tomorrow...' he
murmured to her in passing again, when hunger drove
her to make a beeline for the banqueting hall.

Escort in tow, she paused in the doorway, took in the
vast and colourful array of food and the scarlet-liveried
flunkeys, and slowly turned to István, her appetite suddenly ruined.

'I very much doubt that tomorrow could be worse than
today,' she said quietly.

'Doubt no longer. It could,' he answered meaningfully.

Her teeth ground together. She'd need extended dental
treatment if he stayed around, taunting her! 'We've got
to talk,' she said with a stiff reluctance. Heaving a sigh
of resignation, she decided that somehow she'd get a
promise of good behaviour from István if it was the last
thing she did. Managing a brave smile, she touched her
escort's arm. 'Thank you—*Köszönöm*,' she said warmly.
He took the hint. With a low bow and a kiss of Tanya's
hand, he left her side with some reluctance. 'At least
some of your countrymen have manners,' she told István
pointedly.

'We're rather special people.'

'You aside, I'd have to be deaf, dumb and blind not
to agree,' she retorted. Warmth had crept into her voice
and a smile of far-away sweetness touched her lips.
'Everyone's so hospitable and friendly that it's made this
evening bearable.'

'More than that, I hope. We're the most interesting people in the world.'

Tanya smiled faintly at his biased opinion. Regrettably, he was interesting, though. Her curiosity burned to know what he'd done when he'd first arrived in Hungary; where he'd gone, if he'd known who his family were, and how he'd adapted to the different lifestyle.

'Lisa always raved about the Hungarians,' she mused, then checked herself. Her friend had once raved about István in particular.

'A woman of impeccable taste,' he murmured, laughter in his voice.

'In choosing John?' she parried coolly, knowing he'd been referring to himself. 'Of course. And how clever of him,' she continued, boosting her brother's achievements, 'to get a job here. Someone must have recognised his qualities.'

'Absolutely.'

She flashed the suspiciously agreeable István a quick glance, but he was acknowledging the wave of a grey-haired woman at the far end of the room.

Stick at it, she told herself. There was some headway to be made before they all went to bed. Before István's mind—and body—dwelt on bed and linked it with Lisa. At the moment, he seemed absorbed by the beauties of the frescoed room. He was leaning against a massive carved sideboard that bore dishes of sorbets and ices, chocolate hearts and sweet pastries.

Since he seemed proud of anything Hungarian, she'd plump for keeping the conversation on those lines. And getting a few more digs in. 'Lisa must be proud of John,' she ventured. 'I don't think I've ever been in a more beautiful place. The castle's absolutely perfect for a romantic wedding.'

'He's chosen well. They couldn't have selected anywhere better,' he acknowledged to her surprise. 'This is one of Hungary's most beautiful, most famous mansions,' he said, only half aware of her, it seemed.

'Napoleon ate in this very room,' he said quietly, his eyes soft with pleasure.

'How exciting!' Touched by his pride, she was silent and tried to imagine the castle as it must have been in the past, as the home of some Hungarian noble. 'How do you know about such things as the castle's stock of porcelain and who came here in the past?' she asked suddenly.

'Everyone knows,' he dismissed.

'Oh, really?' She wasn't entirely convinced but wasn't prepared to argue the point. First she had to establish some vaguely tolerable communication between them, then suggest gently that hassling John wasn't worth the effort. So, 'I never expected to feel so comfortable in such a grand place. It must have been quite something in the old days. And now it's a hotel. Awful to have your home overrun by strangers,' she sighed, thinking of the countess.

'Better to have people in it, living, breathing, dancing, enjoying themselves, than to see it destroyed by neglect,' he replied with passionate intensity. 'I expect the countess enjoys the fact that the estate and village have come to life again.'

This was a different István. One she could almost empathise with. 'Do you know anything about her?' she asked hopefully, thinking that she must remind John about his letter of introduction.

He shot her a quick, assessing glance. 'She's one of the Huszár family. They're descended from the Magyars—the nomadic horsemen who settled in Hungary a thousand years ago,' he said casually.

Tanya clasped her hands together in delight. 'More romance! This country is steeped in history. It's quite fascinating.' To her surprise, he didn't scoff at all. Perhaps, she thought, because this is his heritage. She felt a strong sense of pride that she was half Hungarian too and an urgent need to know about her roots. 'Tell me more,' she begged. 'I want to know more. I wish I could stay longer. I must come back.'

His eyes glowed with pleasure and she realised they'd found common ground at last. 'About what?' he asked indulgently.

'Start with the castle. Whatever you know about it. Its past,' she said, her face eager. 'What happened to it in Communist times?'

'I forget you know little about Hungary,' he smiled. 'All the land became State-owned after the Second World War,' he explained. 'It was divided into plots and shared out among the workers.'

'That was good, wasn't it?' she asked. 'Equal rights for the workers.'

'Yes and no. Big estates like this one gradually declined in production because they were so fragmented and consequently less efficient. No one person—including the State—could afford the vast sums necessary to keep the manor houses and castles in good repair. In time the amount of work available decreased and everything went to rack and ruin. It's a situation that was repeated everywhere.'

'What a shame it didn't work. Such a good idea in theory,' she said thoughtfully.

'I feel that these great houses and estates are part of our past, a piece of history,' said István earnestly. 'They should be preserved if possible. Someone had to husband the land, to manage it, to have an overview——'

'Also to provide employment,' she interrupted, 'and give workers on the estate some security of work and tenure——'

'In a humane, caring way.' He smiled at her look of surprise. 'Humane? Caring? I know what you're thinking. That it's a good thing I'm not in charge!' he joked lightly. Her face fell in disappointment. He'd spoilt the mood. 'Almost had a normal conversation there for a moment, didn't we?' he murmured. 'I really must watch that tendency.'

'I wish you'd give more of yourself and your opinions,' she sighed. She'd been enjoying the discussion and for a moment or two had forgotten why she was prompting him to talk.

'Surely you don't care what I think?' he asked, amused. 'Besides, you know I'm not likely to reveal myself. I prefer not to expose my thoughts or feelings to people.'

'Yes, I know. Why?'

'Blunt as always,' he said ruefully. After a moment's hesitation, he said quietly, 'Perhaps it will help if you know. Another veil... It was Ester's ruling from as far back as I remember. It was the way she taught me to behave.'

Tanya's eyes widened. 'Mother? Why should she do that?'

Again, István considered his reply for a moment, studying the shiny toes of his shoes with an impassive expression. 'She knew,' he said slowly, 'that one day, when I was told that I wasn't her child—or your father's—I'd need to leave. She wanted me to walk out without a backward glance.'

'Which you did!' she said, resentment making her mouth sulky.

And he touched it, softly, his finger pressing into the jutting lower lip, making every part of her body come alive. I ache for him, she thought sadly. I hunger for a man I despise.

'My welcome had worn out, I think. You made it clear that I wasn't flavour of the month,' he said drily.

'So now you're accusing me of making you leave?' she cried, her eyes dark with distress. In her bitterness at the way he'd treated Lisa, she'd wanted him to go— had told him he wasn't fit to live in the vicarage, that... She cringed inwardly at the dreadful insults she'd flung at him. And when he'd gone she'd mourned! No one could have been more contrary. 'You never cared what I thought or said,' she said sullenly. 'If you'd wanted to stay, you would have done.'

'Sometimes choices are made for us,' he said quietly and took her elbow in his hand. 'Come with me a moment, Tanya.'

She resisted, not trusting his intentions. 'No. I don't want to.'

'Just to that door and those chairs inside,' he said, a gesture of his head indicating the entrance to a brightly lit conservatory. 'I think I should tell you about Ester.'

'All right, then, tell me here!' she demanded.

'I need your undivided attention and no eaves-droppers,' he said quietly. 'If I had my way, I'd be telling you somewhere totally private, but I'm not wasting my time proposing that. I doubt you'd trust me. But if you want to know about your mother then I suggest you do as I ask.'

She shrugged her assent and let him escort her to the conservatory where he pulled up two large wicker chairs. Silently, consumed with curiosity, she curled up on the cherry-red cushions embroidered with white orchids which echoed the huge clay pots crammed with real or-chids that lined the conservatory shelves. But her sur-roundings barely impinged on her consciousness. When she angled her head enquiringly at István, she saw that he was looking at her intently.

'Well? What about Mother?' she asked, anxious to hear what he had to say.

His hand lifted as though to touch her hair and dropped back to his knee again. 'Poor Tanya,' he said gently. 'I've pushed you a little too far and filled your head with too much to see what's in front of your nose. OK. Let's unravel a little of this tangle. I was telling you that my departure was always on the cards. It had been planned before I was born.'

'By your real mother?' asked Tanya, grudgingly sympathetic.

'I'd stayed in England longer than I should,' he said huskily. 'Ester kept me ignorant of my situation for too long. She should have told me about my background and released me when I reached the age of eighteen. If she had, it would have saved a lot of heartache.'

'That's true,' she said sadly. 'But... I know you've claimed that it had been arranged that you should return to Hungary, but surely it doesn't follow that it was necessary for Mother to withhold all emotion from you while she was bringing you up!' she cried passionately, her hands twisting in her lap.

'I suppose she thought it would help if I wasn't committed to any one person, to any one place,' he said unemotionally.

Tanya looked at him in exasperation. 'If that's true, then Mother was quite wrong to isolate you from us! We could have stayed together as a happy family if she'd brought you up in the general hurly-burly of our house, instead of sending you to posh schools! You could have been our foster brother and more of a friend. I don't understand. There's no law that says someone *has* to go back to the land of their parents' birth! You could have visited them, said hello, got to know them a bit, and come back to us! You could have shared yourself out, between your mother and mine, instead of cutting off all ties!' she wailed. And thought, The waste of it all. The terrible waste.

'Calm down,' he said gently. 'What you're suggesting was out of the question. Ester did what she thought was right to fulfil her duty. She'd given her oath to my mother that one day I would return to Hungary. I was isolated from you all to ensure I never made a close bond with you.'

She was shocked into a numb silence for a while. 'Mother intentionally moulded you into an unfeeling man!' Tanya digested this for a moment. Her mother had mistakenly crushed his capacity for love, denied him the pleasure of family life. She felt a surge of deep pity for him. 'I'm sure she didn't realise what she was doing,' she husked.

'You're wrong. She knew perfectly well what she was doing. She felt it would be wrong to love me.'

Tanya cringed at his cold, matter-of-fact tone. Her darling mother had produced a monster with no heart. How sad that István had never known her mother's love! Was that why she'd guiltily lavished money on him instead?

'This is a lesson to me. When I marry,' she said shakily, 'it'll be to a man who's sensitive and loving and not afraid to show his feelings! And our children will be loved equally—and treated equally—from the word go!'

István looked strained. 'I hope you find a man like that,' he said gruffly. 'I know you'll make a wonderful wife and mother.'

The unexpected compliment made her flinch. Sadly she wondered at her chances of finding the right man. And whether she and István would both be alone, unloved, for the rest of their lives. 'Thank you,' she said stiffly. 'You learn a lot from the way your parents bring you up, don't you? Their mistakes...' She bit her lip. Her mother's mistake had been to treat István differently and she was still coming to terms with the fact that her mother had been largely responsible for his behaviour. 'Was it a shock when she told you about your background, or did you suspect something?' she asked anxiously.

'It was a shock,' he said shortly. 'I didn't believe her at first. But the moment she told me, several things fell into place, and all the time I was denying what she said I knew in my heart that she was speaking the truth.'

Her eyes filled with a helpless compassion. 'I can understand that. I think you would have been different from us however you'd been brought up. When—when did you know?' she asked gently.

The bones in his face seemed more prominent than ever. 'After you all but dragged me off my horse by King Arthur's Crag and screamed at me like a banshee,' he growled.

That had been immediately after she'd left Lisa recovering from losing his baby at the hospital. What a terrible day! Such a coincidence, too, that her mother

should have chosen that difficult moment to reveal her
secret to István.

'I screamed at you because Lisa was——' she began,
and found her wrist enclosed in steel.

'I know,' he said grimly. 'Lisa could have been
seriously damaged by what happened, physically, mentally, emotionally. I was fully aware of the potential
consequences. The doctor told me she might have died
if she had tried to cope on her own and had delayed
calling you. You don't have to spell out the seriousness
of it all to me.'

'But still you went off riding instead of staying by her
bedside!' she accused.

'What could I do?' he asked roughly. 'The doctor said
I had to let her sleep. And I took the opportunity to
think and let off some——' He checked himself. 'I was
concerned,' he said in a low tone. 'I've never stopped
being concerned for her.'

Tanya winced. 'I thought that was so,' she said huskily.

'I'm afraid that incident has affected her,' he frowned.
'She's wary of love, wary of trusting anyone.'

Tanya thought, He knows Lisa isn't sure of her love
for John. He'll take advantage of that! 'You'd admit
that it was irresponsible for a man of the world to seduce
an innocent and trusting young girl, then,' she said
shakily.

'Oh, yes. In the extreme. That day is engraved in my
memory,' he said with soft savagery. 'I hate thinking of
it. I wish I could forget it, everything that happened!'

'Poor Lisa,' she said fervently.

Reaching out, he plucked an orchid and tucked it in
her hair. 'You look pale. When did you last eat
anything?'

'Breakfast-time, and only a slice of toast then,' she
admitted. 'I—I didn't feel like anything on the plane.'
Her nerves had churned up her stomach too much. 'I
think I'd better have something now.' Perhaps her woozy
head would be better afterwards, she thought. 'Will you
tell me the rest of the story, though?' she asked anxiously.

It was important that she understand him if she was to understand his motives towards Lisa and deflect his purpose.

'I need a little time, the right moment, the right setting,' he answered with a bland smile.

'But——!'

'No. Not now. Later,' he said in a tone that brooked no denial.

She groaned, but knew it would be impossible to get any more out of him until he was ready. So she accepted his offered hand and returned to the banqueting-room.

To her mind, the array of food would have sunk Napoleon and the whole of his French army if they'd marched in at that moment. It was a feast of lavish splendour, far grander than anything John could afford. Why hadn't that occurred to her before? This wedding must be costing a fortune! She'd willingly lent John a good deal of the money she'd saved so that he could come over and woo Lisa. Since he'd only recently landed the job managing the hotel, surely he couldn't have paid for the extravagant banquet?

'Do you know if this is a very expensive hotel?' she asked anxiously.

'It's pretty exclusive,' he answered with a private smile, handing her a crested plate.

Surreptitiously, she let her fingers touch the flower garlands which hung in swags along the endless buffet table. Real ivy. Real orchids! The huge gold bows were made not from ribbon but some rich brocade, the stiffly starched tablecloth was edged with gold and entwined hearts. She hoped John hadn't got into debt to impress his bride.

Perhaps the food was cheap. Each dish was labelled in Hungarian and English and the names made her smile. '"Bridegroom soup"'?' Laughter wiped away her frown.

'Old Hungarian dish,' he assured her solemnly.

'What about that one? "Catch-a-man stew"! Some-one's got a sense of humour!'

'Local fare,' he chuckled. 'In the old days, a young woman's cooking skills were displayed to a prospective bridegroom by food like this. He'd be invited to taste a meal she'd cooked and I presume if he liked it he might begin to court her.'

'The way to a man's heart...?' she suggested ruefully. 'Are you telling me that marriage was based on whether or not a woman could produce a rib-sticking stew?' Her eyes dancing in amusement, she was looking forward to arguing her corner.

István laughed. 'Nothing's changed. Women then and now make the selection first and last, while men make all the running in between. Men are the mere pawns in their hands.'

'You included?' she grinned. 'I can see you letting a woman dictate all the moves, playing a minor role and obediently doing what you're told!'

'Now chess is a very subtle game,' he said, ladling wine-rich meat on to his capacious plate. 'It's hard to tell which particular move changes the whole outcome. One false move can ruin brilliant play——'

'It's a very Hungarian skill, isn't it, playing chess?' she mused idly.

He beamed. 'Yes. Very Hungarian.' He sampled an elaborately plaited pastry stuffed with chicken. 'So's this. You must try some.' He held out his fork.

Without even hesitating, she let her mouth close around the morsel. 'Mmm! *Gorgeous*!' Perhaps the old saying was true, she thought wryly. The way to a man's heart was through his stomach. István had relaxed a great deal. They were on quite good terms now. 'These dishes go on forever! I do hope John gets a discount or he'll be paying for this for the rest of his life!' she commented.

'No,' István said absently. 'No discount. And don't worry, he didn't pay a penny.'

She started. 'How on earth do you know?' He tapped his nose knowingly. 'Tell me!' she urged. 'I'm worried. It can't have been Lisa—she's not even finished her music studies. She wouldn't have the money to provide such a feast.'

'I wonder who, then?' he murmured. 'Lisa's parents are dead, your father never had any money because of his boundless charity, Sue's ploughing everything into her business, Mariann's lifestyle in London is expensive. Now who else, I wonder,' murmured István in the tone of a man who knew, 'cares enough to lay on a spread for Lisa? A benefactor? Someone who cares for her——'

Her heart began to thud at his smug expression. 'Not...oh, no, István! Not *you*!'

'Guilty. Don't you like me helping your friend out?' he enquired.

'Not in the circumstances, no,' she frowned.

'Someone had to. I offered, she accepted. I'm glad you're trying the "Thieves' bite",' he said as she dazedly lifted a skewer of meat and potato from a vast dish.

'Thieves' bite'! she thought grimly, not seeing any label with that name. The man was too inventive for words. With disdain—and reluctance, since it looked tempting—she deposited the skewer firmly on his plate.

'You can't be that rich or that generous,' she said tartly.

'Can't I?'

She had rated him before only in the handsome stakes. This time, she rated him for wealth. Her eyes took in his confident air, the perfectly groomed head, well-cut hair and hand-fitted dinner-jacket. The shirt looked expensive, his heavy watch was a gold Rolex and, now she came to think of it, the chefs behind the tables had been particularly watchful and deferential towards him.

He was pointing to a dish of paprika and chatting in a friendly but slightly reserved way to the chef, who, on István's instructions, was bringing the silver bowl nearer to the edge of the table so that guests could reach it more easily. That was more than arrogance. It was the self-assurance of a man who wielded money or authority—

or both—with such a sure touch that he carried an aura of power around with him.

'So you're rich,' she said curtly, wondering how. He hadn't had a penny four years ago. His family? She dismissed the idea out of hand. No wealthy family would consider handing their son over to a homely, ordinary woman like her mother.

'I've made a packet,' he told her, supplying the answer.

'You always were clever,' she said grudgingly. 'Despite the fact that you played truant loads of times, you still managed to pass any exam you wanted to. Are you using your business degree?'

She'd hated it when he'd come home for holidays while he was at university. He'd been so rude. And he'd been even worse when he worked as an events promotor, negotiating with the media to get top coverage for major equestrian events. They'd fought like cat and dog and he'd given up living at home altogether, camping in a horsebox and whizzing about the countryside in a BMW. A yuppie gypsy, she'd called him.

'I keep busy.' His hand brushed the side of her cheek in what would have been an affectionate gesture in anyone else. This was calculated to annoy her, however, and put her on edge; she knew that too well. 'Little dreamer!' he murmured. 'What a muddle you are! Were those glazed eyes of yours thinking about your adolescence, or our passionate session in your room?'

Tanya squirmed at the truth and recovered herself with difficulty. 'I was thinking of what you must have done to get rich,' she said, blindly picking up three forks and then replacing them in confusion at his low chuckle and wondering which question to ask first. 'So you're rolling in it. But why would you lay out money on Lisa's reception?'

'Guilt?' he suggested, his eyebrows lifting sardonically.

'When did guilt ever bother *you*?' she scoffed. But inside her head a nagging voice told her that there was no other explanation. Unless he was very, very fond of Lisa and wanting to show her how rich he was, how generous he could be to a woman. Absently she lifted a slice of goose and then pheasant on to her laden plate.

There was the shadowy hint of a smile on his cynical lips. 'Lisa's enormously grateful,' he volunteered. 'Your mouth's open. Want it closed? I know a fun way.'

She did it herself, fast, her hands itching to slap his face. A jittery nerve wiggled at the corner of her mouth. 'This spread must have cost thousands!' she said in worried tones. 'I can't accept for a moment that you felt *that* guilty.'

'You're right,' he sighed. 'Seen through me again! OK. I come clean. I had an ulterior motive. But I think I'll get a good return on my investment,' he said easily.

'What?' she cried belligerently, the food almost sliding to the floor in her agitation.

'Lisa keeps thanking me.' The cynicism briefly gave way to a disarming innocence. 'Says she doesn't know what she can do to repay me! I told her I'd think of something.'

Tanya's knees shook. 'Are you telling me that you did this on the expectation that Lisa would return your favour?' she squeaked.

István shrugged. 'Subtle, eh? That's up to her. Do you think she might?'

Sexual blackmail? He lived in a different world, she thought, aghast. Behaviour like that didn't figure in the normal daily life of Widecombe village! Stunned by his total lack of morals, Tanya felt her numb body being pushed along by the increased crush of people, and she moved along on auto-pilot, thoughts racing through her head.

Lisa had let István wind her around his little finger before—and look what trouble that had caused! Tonight, he was all too obviously intending to inject a bit of fun into his jaded lifestyle by calling on Lisa's gratitude. It was too horrible to contemplate.

Jerking her head around and muttering softly under her breath, she muttered, 'You want to make love——'

'To you. Yes, I do. Nice to think that the "Catch-a-man stew" works even from a distance,' he said blandly. 'Now you've made the first move, shall we take our food and go feast upstairs and do some moving together?'

Slowly she lowered her plate, her whole body running amok and saying *yes*. Appalled, she registered that his hand was on her small, high rear. . . sliding to the dip in her back, the swell of her hip, the curve of her tiny waist, and she yearned to turn, slip her hands around his neck and feel the pressure of his lips on hers.

'Stop, please stop! Someone will see!' she hissed jerkily.

'*Fogdoss*!' he whispered. 'It means "Take your hands off me". You might need it in the next few hours.'

'Why?' she asked, afraid of the answer. '*Fog—fog—* something!' she said desperately, a fog definitely descending on her brain.

His body came firmly against hers, the movement disguised by the crowd all around them. To her thorough disgust, she was loving the very feel of him, the hardness of his chest, its warmth and strength, the pressure of his hipbone. Without meaning to, she inhaled the faint elusive muskiness of him and fought the urge to press her body passionately against his. Hastily, to give herself something else to do, she reached out for a flute of champagne and downed it on a long swallow before it dawned on her that she could have thrown it at him if she'd only had her wits about her.

'Getting a little tense, are we?' he murmured insolently.

Warm hands caressed her shoulders, burning her flesh. She'd never felt like this in her life before. Some devil was willing her to abandon all propriety and respond but she knew that if she gave one small hint, or the slightest gesture that she found his touch desirable, he'd set off an explosion within her that would take a week sitting up to her neck in the Danube to cool down.

'Only because everyone thinks you're my brother,' she rasped jerkily, pressing against the banqueting table to avoid the intimacy of his pelvis against her tingling buttocks. 'Don't behave like my lover!'

'I can't help touching you,' he said huskily, nuzzling her ear on the pretence of whispering a brotherly secret in it. She shuddered and he let out a low, throaty growl of hunger. 'The tragedy of man. And the downfall of woman,' he breathed.

'What is?' she asked shakily, knowing he was leading up to something.

István's hand reached to her chin and he tipped it around so that she was forced to look at his mocking eyes. 'Sex,' he said simply. 'Adam and Eve. You ought to read our celebrated Imre Madách on the subject of man's aspirations, but I suppose you won't have time tonight.'

'Why?' she asked thickly.

His eyes glittered. 'Isn't that self-evident?'

'N-no!' she breathed, her ability to reason things out sticking stubbornly on the 'stop' button.

'Then let me spell it out for you. You'll be far too busy listening for erotic sounds in the room next to yours,' he said lazily, taking her elbow firmly and leading her away. 'Or making them yourself.'

Her stomach lurched. 'I-I don't intend to let you make love to me and I don't for one minute think Lisa will spend tonight with you either.' She refused to dwell on the thought of István and Lisa together. With considerable hauteur, she stalked down the middle of the room, István at her shoulder every step of the way. Her nerves were in shreds. She couldn't stand him another second. 'Go and pester someone else!' she hissed, grim-faced.

He sighed extravagantly. 'I'm not too good at coping with rejection. It makes me rush elsewhere for comfort so someone else can heal my bruised ego. Well, what do you know!' he said, without pausing for breath. 'There's Lisa.' A wicked light in his eyes, he smiled and waved as Lisa headed to the ballroom, her violin in her hand. Tanya felt a horrifying lurch in her stomach at the way

Lisa's face lit up like a beacon. 'Since there's nothing doing here, I'll see if she's more user-friendly——'

'No!' Tanya gritted her teeth, wondering how she could do a U-turn and persuade him to stay with her when only seconds ago she'd tried to send him off with a flea in his ear. 'I—I want you to tell me more about Mother and about yourself,' she said stiffly, unable to give him any other safe explanation for her change of heart.

'Do you really?' he said. She fumed. His self-satisfied, mocking smile suggested she was using that as a way of accepting his invitation for sex. 'Do you want us to chat cosily upstairs, after I've made mad, passionate love to you——?'

'Down here!' she snapped, feeling the hysteria rising again. 'We eat, we listen to the music and you talk to me like a brother!'

'And *then* we go upstairs,' he said silkily. 'No, don't protest. I'm confident you will, if you care about John's happiness.'

She stumbled, her feet suddenly as weak as the rest of her body at the menace he'd injected into that final sentence. 'What does that crack mean? Are you trying to blackmail me too?' she grated.

'No. Succeeding.'

The threat was in every confident line of his body. She gasped, her hand touching her breast. 'What...?' Her voice ran out. He'd placed his hand tenderly over hers, smiling into her eyes with an intense affection that rocketed right through her. She found her emotions overwhelming. Too deep for her to understand. The thought of making love with him filled her with joy, not shame. She *knew* he was bad, through and through, but something else was telling her that there was more beyond that mocking exterior and if she could only find it she'd be content.

Which was a ridiculous thought, of course, because dozens of women had probably had the same feeling and ended up on the scrap heap.

'Careful,' he murmured. 'Your pheasant is heading for the floor.'

'Oh, dear!' she said feebly, levelling her plate. It shook in her hands, and all because István was giving one of his 'I'm available, fly me' smiles! 'I think it was taking cover,' she said ruefully.

He laughed. 'Must be a hunter around somewhere with his sights trained on you.'

She made a face. 'I'm anti-blood-sports.'

'We could compromise,' he grinned. 'Settle for enjoying the chase and the celebratory get-together afterwards.'

He looked so handsome and carefree, she mused wistfully, that she wanted the banter to go on forever. Instead she knew she'd have to tackle him head-on soon. And that she was putting off that moment.

Dimly she was aware that the dance music had changed in the ballroom and Lisa had begun to play with a small group of her fellow music students. István led Tanya to a small table and sat down to listen to the string quartet.

'I've heard this before,' she said slowly. István leaned back in his chair, his eyes fixed intently on Lisa's flushed, fair face as she took her solo.

'Liszt and Bartok and Kodály,' he said with satisfaction. 'Lisa's good. She interprets their music with the soul of a truly passionate woman.'

Tanya winced. 'I heard that tune when Mother shut herself up in the study with you.'

His eyes glittered. 'Yes. Why did she do that? You were half Hungarian; she never played it to you.'

Tanya shrugged. 'I don't know. I suppose because she'd promised your real mother that you'd go back to Hungary. And you would need to know about your heritage,' she said slowly. 'Like the language—you learnt the language, the culture, probably, too. If you were going back you'd need to integrate——'

'Why?' he asked, leaning forward intently.

Tanya frowned. 'Just to make it easier. Did you find your mother?'

'Yes. Isn't Lisa beautiful?' he said softly, his eyes on the small figure on the dais.

Tanya's heart turned somersaults. 'Lovely. And spoken for,' she reminded him apprehensively. He continued to watch Lisa with burning, passionate eyes and all the while Tanya's pulses were racing faster and faster. 'Don't hurt her!' she begged miserably. She felt her hand enclosed in his fierce grip.

'This is promising,' he remarked softly. 'You're getting increasingly desperate. You care for your friend very much, don't you? How far would you go to protect her?'

'A long way—but...' She shut her mouth quickly.

'The long way sounds good. Tell me,' he said in a voice so low that she found herself leaning forwards to hear him, 'would you say I was a highly sexed man?'

Her tongue moistened her lips and she swallowed before she managed to answer. 'Over-sexed.'

'Such is a man's reputation!' he murmured. 'Then you'll accept that I'll need a woman in my bed tonight,' he said, his mouth soft and sultry. 'The question is, who will it be?'

Tanya froze. She was way ahead of him. Her mouth opened but no sound came out and she was aware that István's hot eyes were scalding her lips with their intensity. 'You mean ... You're saying it has to be either L-Lisa ... or ... me?' she croaked eventually.

'Clever girl. Think about it. It's within your power to save her from my evil clutches. I don't mind either way. You or her.' His face filled her vision, sensuality flowed from his smouldering eyes and poured into her dismayingly receptive body. 'Will you sacrifice yourself for her? It would be quite a test of your loyalty to her and John,' he murmured softly, drawing a shudderingly gentle finger down the side of her face.

And he left her, strolling across the dance-floor while she stared after him, as cold as ice and utterly stunned by the choice he'd given her.

CHAPTER FIVE

SHAKING from head to toe, Tanya took several sips of her champagne and found the flute was empty. So she absently picked up István's. The bubbles fizzed on her nose and she slowly concentrated on the sensation. Anything rather than think about the dilemma she was in.

Enviously she watched a laughing Mariann running across the floor to join a group of admiring men. Sue was deep in conversation with a man in a beautifully embroidered jacket. If only she were carefree and happy like her sisters, with their capacity for enjoying life! Nothing seemed to trouble them. Whereas she...

Tanya toyed with the slender stem of her glass, tears blurring her vision. István had always been particularly brutal towards her. Why? She glared in his direction and met his amused eyes. A little late, she was beginning to recognise his technique now. He liked to hit below the belt, slip away to a vantage point where he could enjoy watching her writhe for a while, then slip back and slug her silly again.

Resentfully she watched him stride across the floor and ask some unsuspecting female to dance. A gypsy violinist, with eyes as intense as István's, had taken over from the classical string quartet and was playing an infectious tune that brought everyone on to the floor.

Watching István begin the complex folk dance, Tanya felt desire creep like a thief back into her body. The dance was hot and fiery, with plenty of foot-stamping and hand-clapping, and István had undone the button on his dinner-jacket so that it was flying open, his face alive and filled with a feverish excitement.

She was on the edge of her chair, tingling in the most unlikely places as the music and István's response to it reached inside her and touched a chord that vibrated throughout her body. She knew why she found him so utterly irresistible; he energised her, filled her with passion and the frightening knowledge that she could be alive for the first time if only she threw away all inhibitions and...

Was she mad? It was out of the question!

Unfortunately.

Pale with strain, fighting the lure of the recklessly rousing music, she ate the meal in front of her, the spicy dishes blending into cardboard in her unreceptive mouth. And then, after repeated entreaties, she danced, laughing brightly again to fool everyone. But all the time she was aware that István had drawn Lisa into a corner and was talking earnestly, passionately to her, his hand resting on her knee, his eyes fixed mesmerically on hers.

'Tan. Do something about István!' hissed John when she returned, exhausted, to her seat. 'You said you'd take care of him! If I as much as speak to him, I'm likely to sock him on the jaw and Lisa will never forgive me.'

Reluctantly she followed the jerk of John's head to where his bride-to-be was engrossed in intimate isolation with an unusually tender-looking István. Controlling the leap of her pulses, she sighed and realised that John was right. He mustn't drive Lisa into István's arms.

Marching over purposefully, she touched Lisa's shoulder lightly. 'Enough gas-bagging; time István and I had a dance,' she said bossily, creaking her mouth into an inviting smile.

'No, thanks. I want to talk to Lisa,' said István smugly, and rocked back in his chair, folding his arms as if to say, Coax me.

She swallowed a rude retort and wagged her finger at him. 'Lisa has a duty to *all* her guests,' she trilled. An idea came to her. 'You've had plenty of chances to be together over the past year.'

'He told you?' exclaimed Lisa, surprised.

She'd been right! A year together! Tanya stiffened.

'We haven't met *that* often,' drawled István, his eyes narrowed. 'I'm a pretty busy man. Often enough, though,' he added.

Tanya hastily turned her gasp into a sigh. '*Do* come and dance!' she pleaded, an edge of desperation in her tone. 'People will wonder why you're not paying your eldest *sister* any attention.'

He frowned and she bristled to think that he should prefer Lisa's company to hers. Idiot! she scolded herself furiously. 'I suppose I'll have to,' he said with great reluctance. 'Can't be churlish. We'll continue this later, sweetheart,' he added in a fond murmur to Lisa.

'Continue what?' Tanya asked suspiciously, when he'd swept her into his arms. Too late, she discovered that they were dancing a tango and wished it had been something with less body contact, like a Highland reel. Or tennis. This was turning out to be closer to mouth-to-mouth resuscitation!

For a moment, István bent her right back, forcing her supple body to obey him till her hair swept the floor, his wickedly handsome face hovering dramatically over hers. 'I think Lisa's getting cold feet about the wedding,' he murmured, and whipped her back upright before she could reply, whirling her into a fast, cheek-to-cheek stride down the length of the ballroom.

Cold feet! she thought dizzily, trying to keep a hold on the conversation. All those flicks of his hands, the push of his hips were a deliberate attempt to confuse her. No one else was hurtling up and down as fast as they were!

'Cold feet are OK. All brides get them,' she said, wildly generalising. 'Must be those satin slippers they insist on wearing.' There was a satin feel to the warm slide of his cheek and it tantalised her unmercifully. The closeness of his mouth curved in a way that was unfairly desirable to her lowered eyes.

He chuckled. 'Hers are particularly frost-bitten, poor darling,' he said fondly. 'She has so many doubts——'

'About what?' breathed Tanya in alarm.

'Her emotions.'

'No!' she moaned. Her body went limp in his arms and she had to grab him tightly because he'd swept her to the ground again to the sound of clapping. 'Stop showing off!' she muttered in embarrassment. 'We're not Torvill and Dean! Where was I?'

'At an angle of forty-five degrees, denying what incredible partners we are and mumbling something about ice-skaters,' he said helpfully.

'Lisa. Her emotions,' she gritted through her teeth.

'Turn that grimace into a grin. She's looking worried.'

Obligingly, for Lisa's sake, she flashed a dazzling smile at István that left her eyes like shards of glass. 'She doesn't know how worried she ought to be,' she muttered. 'You encouraged her doubts, I suppose,' she said bitterly.

'No. I didn't have to. But I did wonder,' he mused, 'whether to take it into my head to take pity on her and rub her cold feet back into life somewhere private.'

'You won't have a chance to!'

'Oh, are we "on", then?' he enquired innocently.

'No, we are not "on", as you so disgustingly put it! I'm going to sit with her all night,' said Tanya triumphantly. 'That'll stop you bothering either of us!'

'I have a feeling she'll be less than thrilled,' drawled István. His eyes narrowed and she followed his gaze to see Lisa and a tense-backed John disappearing into the garden. 'Love's the very devil, isn't it? Pleasure and pain. Is it worth it, I wonder? Those two have quite a lot to work out before tomorrow morning,' he commented drily.

She tried to wrench herself away but he held her in a grip of iron. 'You snake! You poisonous, venemous snake! I've got your measure!' she seethed.

'I doubt it. No one can measure a live snake,' he chuckled. 'Don't imagine that you can outwit me,' he continued, infuriatingly self-assured. 'I'm several moves ahead of you. I've got it all planned out.'

'And I,' she said, filled with an extraordinary excitement at the prospect, 'will block every move you make!'

'What fun!' he murmured and she frowned, wondering why she thought so too. 'I'm delighted. Your tenacity is admirable. I must say, you look far more effervescent and alive than when I first saw you,' he smiled.

'I enjoy a challenge,' she explained huskily.

'I know. That's why I'm giving you one,' he laughed.

She smiled wryly. Into her conscious mind came the sound of the gypsy singing huskily, adding a rawly sensual layer to the passionate music. The man's eyes twinkled at her and she found herself smiling in return. Around her, the dancers began to whoop and cheer with delight as the song became throatier and the accompanying violin music faster.

Filled with inexplicable elation and an urge to abandon herself to the revels, she knew she ought to get away from István before she shed too many defences, but knew she couldn't. Besides, while she danced with him, she consoled herself, at least Lisa and John were safe.

'Smile like that, glow like that, and you'll have every man here falling in love with you,' said István huskily. 'The gypsies are already smitten.'

The trio of musicians in their embroidered waistcoats and baggy black trousers were bearing down on them and quickly surrounded her, their lively faces sparkling with mischief as they intensified the rhythm. Despite herself, she laughed because the men were suffused with joy and she let them whisk her into a wild dance before they returned her to István. Driven by a need to let out some of her feelings, she kissed them all impulsively to roars of approval.

'That was wonderful!' she said fervently.

'And that was a nice gesture.' He hesitated, and then, 'Goddammit, you really are the most beautiful woman I've ever seen!' he growled.

Subduing the euphoria within her, she stared at him with saucer-like eyes. 'I—I got a bit carried away. I was having a good time,' she said huskily.

'The *csárdás*,' he smiled, 'is pretty wild.'

'Chardash,' she repeated softly, pleased to learn another word.

'Hungarians are supposed to have temperaments that swing from the joyful to the melancholic,' he told her. 'Stay with the joy. It suits you. After all, you're half Hungarian.'

'Yes...' Her eyes sparkled. 'I am, I am! Dance with me again!' she said recklessly as the music scattered all thought of leaving the dance-floor. 'I can't keep my feet still.'

István's laughter lit his face. He pulled her into his arms and she gave herself to the music inside her, abandoning her more sedate self. For now, she wanted to dance till she dropped.

'Faster?'

Tanya threw her head back to meet his dark eyes boldly. 'Why not?' she cried and he whirled her into such an energetic and physically demanding series of movements that there was no room in her head for anything but an uninhibited excitement as sound and rhythm swirled through her veins.

'This is the way to live!' growled István huskily in her ear.

Laughter and music filled the air and suddenly she felt as light as air. 'Yes! I mean...this is fun!' she amended, and sought to explain. 'My best friend is marrying my brother—his childhood sweetheart. They'll settle their doubts, István,' she assured him. 'I'm happy,' she sighed. 'My sisters and I are having a taste of Hungary—which I'm falling in love with. The music is wonderful. I love the whole-hearted way everyone celebrates, I love the castle, I love being here.'

'Listen,' he said gently, 'they've switched moods.' He paused and her eyes were transfixed by the expression of tenderness on his face as he listened to the heartrending folk song. 'When a peasant or a gypsy sings in Hungary,' he continued, smiling at her enchanted expression, 'he generally uses chest notes. That makes the sound intensely passionate and soulful. And that,' he added in his rich, warm voice, 'is why it's hitting us both in the solar plexus.'

He was too perceptive for her liking. He was right. It was affecting her. Perhaps it was her Hungarian blood that made the plaintive, poignant song reach into her heart. Whatever the reason, she felt very sad and emotional even though a few moments ago she'd been elated.

'Darn it!' she muttered. A huge tear had slid from each eye.

'Don't worry,' he said sympathetically, his forefinger dabbing her damp cheekbones. 'You're not the only one to be visibly affected. There are quite a few handkerchiefs wafting around. You're only getting in touch with your roots. We're a nation of extremes, with the capacity to feel desperately sad, or wildly happy. Decadant or frugal, angry or placid; we can be all those in a matter of moments. Emotion reaches us quickly, you see.'

'You included?' she asked wryly.

'Maybe I'm the exception. After all, I *was* brought up in England, in an English public school,' he smiled. 'My countrymen, however, had none of those disadvantages. They lurch from delight to melancholy whenever they feel like it. It's a country of extremes. Decadance or Communism. Enthusiasm or lethargy. We have a saying here you'll appreciate: We fall to the other side of the horse.'

She gave a small laugh, grateful for the diversion. 'I like that!'

'Does it help you to understand us—and yourself, perhaps?' he asked quietly, his eyes watchful.

She met his warming gaze. There was a sweetness in his face that reminded her of the old days. 'It explains why you were moody as a young man,' she replied.

He went quiet. 'All the time I was in Widecombe I felt *wrong*. It frustrated me that everyone else seemed at ease with their surroundings and the kind of lives they were leading.'

'Mother was happy there,' she observed. 'Yet it must have been quite a wrench for her to start afresh in a strange country.'

'She fell in love soon after she arrived,' he pointed out.

'And she had you. How did she get here? Were you a baby then?'

'I was a few months old. You heard the story when you were small that she'd escaped over the Hungarian border to Germany with the help of freedom fighters. It was quite a risk using forged papers and so on. If she'd been stopped, I suppose she would have been in a lot of trouble with the Communist authorities.'

'Was your real mother dead?' she asked gently.

'No. But for various reasons I was in danger. And she wanted her child to live. Better away from her, in a free country, than dead in her arms.'

'Oh, István!' she cried, her sentimental nature touched by his story. 'Your poor mother! What a sacrifice!'

'Would you have acted so selflessly for the sake of your child, Tanya?' he asked softly.

'Oh, yes, yes!' she said with passion. 'But I'd have demanded that my child was *loved*! Where is your mother now? You said——'

'Hell!' he muttered under his breath.

For a moment, she thought she'd touched on something painful to him. Then her eyes widened in alarm when she saw what had made him tense every muscle in his body. Lisa had run in from the garden, her face composed, but...frozen like a mask. Something was very wrong. Faster than she to react, István jumped up and politely but firmly made his way through the dancers towards Lisa.

By the time Tanya had worked her way out of the ballroom, it was to see the two of them going up the stairs and she realised that Lisa was heading for danger. Any woman was in trouble when István was within striking distance of a bedroom. She took her shoes off, hitched her skirts up and ran.

'No, István!' she cried in a heartfelt plea, horrified to see him stop outside the bridal suite. 'Lisa, don't risk letting him——!'

Guiltily, her friend spun around, then, with a sob, fled inside her room and slammed the door violently.

'Damn! Lisa! Let me in, sweetheart!' muttered István with soft urgency.

'Come away! Leave her alone!' seethed Tanya, her heart bumping away. 'Don't you see you've done enough damage for tonight?'

'Go away!' yelled Lisa.

István cursed. He tried the handle but it was locked. 'Damn!' he repeated, glaring at the door. 'I'll be back later. I have a phone call to make.'

Open-mouthed, Tanya watched him striding away purposefully as though his call took priority over his attempt to get into Lisa's room. 'Lisa! Lisa!' she shouted, hammering on the door. 'I must warn you——'

'Go *away!*' yelled Lisa furiously.

Tanya gave up. At least a disaster had been averted. Shakily she went into her own room, leaving her door ajar so that she could see the corridor. Then she curled up on the bed and listened for when István returned. To her dismay, she heard the sound of a telephone ringing and knew that István must be talking to Lisa, perhaps persuading her to meet him, coaxing her...

Tanya stiffened. Lisa was crying. She pounded on the door again but despite repeated entreaties her friend refused to open it. Back on her bed again, Tanya waited. Her eyes stayed glued to the corridor outside, and she wondered miserably if István would return. After a while the soft sobbing became muffled by the jolly farewells of the guests and finally the distant roar of male voices in the rumpus room where John's stag party was in full swing.

Longing for sleep, she kept her unhappy vigil, forcing herself to stay awake. In the circumstances, it was the best she could do.

Perhaps she did sleep. Something woke her, and she realised it was the castle bell tolling the hour. Two o'clock. She groaned. Stiff and cold, her eyes drooping, she went to the open window and leaned out for a blast of cold night air.

Something flipped out of Lisa's window next door and uncoiled in a blur of white. Astonished, Tanya saw it was a twisted length of silk curtain which had been skilfully knotted into a makeshift rope.

She leaned out, gripping the windowsill. As the flower fell from her hair to the terrace below, her tired mind struggled with the inescapable truth.

Lisa was running away.

Tanya peered out from the clipped yew tree on the edge of the terrace, her breath harsh from running, her chest tight with despair. Mercifully she could see that Lisa was still in her room, partially outlined at the edge of the window.

A sigh of relief whispered from Tanya's dry lips. She'd done the right thing, had come to the right decision. If she'd yelled at Lisa through the locked door she would have woken half the guests—and perhaps hastened Lisa's escape down the rope. If she'd shouted out of her window as Lisa slid to the ground she wouldn't have been able to stop her either.

At least this way Lisa's stupid behaviour might be stopped without anyone knowing. There would be a terrible row between them—but anything was better than the alternative. If Lisa vanished on the eve of her wedding, there would be all hell to pay! And she, Tanya, would be picking up the pieces, she thought gloomily.

How *could* Lisa do this? It was so irresponsible. If she'd realised she didn't love John then she should have faced him with that fact, not scurried off to hide.

Her anxious eyes surveyed the length of the rope. What did one do? Throw a suitcase down first? The whole scenario was awesome. Lisa must be pretty desperate.

'Curse you, István, for putting doubts in her mind!' she grated, joggling up and down to keep warm. Her bare feet felt frozen already on the cold stone.

The figure in the bedroom moved, revealing shoulders broader than Lisa possessed. Shorter hair. Tanya stopped breathing while her eyes opened as wide as they'd go. A man, her confused mind registered! A man, in Lisa's room!

John. It was John...! 'Hope springs eternal', she thought with bitter self-mockery, because of course John wasn't that bulky. She refused to contemplate the other possibility. The unmistakably caressing murmur of a male voice drifted down from the open window. A black riding boot emerged.

She blinked. István had been in a D.J. She drew in her breath sharply and the colour drained slowly from her face. Another man! One who'd climbed into Lisa's room and made her cry. A chill iced her spine. A thug. A... rapist—about to escape.

Tanya knew that help was too far away. The man would be haring across the lawn before she could reach anyone. It was all up to her. A weapon—she needed...something... Her eyes searched frantically and lit on a bundle of stakes, left over from the erection of a marquee on the lawn. Perfect. One swipe in a highly personal place, she thought grimly, and he'd be disabled!

Nervously she tiptoed across the open terrace to the bundle and crouched down, frantically fumbling with the knots on the binder twine. But behind her she heard the slither of body on silk, feet landing on the ground and a silence so profound that it lifted every hair on the back of her neck.

In sheer terror, she straightened slowly, clutching the stake like grim death, her body now prickling with sweat at the sound of leather boots creaking in a steady, measured tread towards her.

Surprise, she thought wildly. She must rely on surprise!

Whirling around with the speed of lightning, she growled fiercely, 'Spread flat on the ground, or——!'

'After you,' drawled István, inviting her with a sweep of his hand to lie at his booted feet.

The stake dropped from her lifeless fingers as her uncomprehending brain tried to make sense of the thug's identity. 'István?' she whispered, bewildered because he was dressed entirely in black, the loose, circus-rider's shirt emphasising the skin-tight riding breeches.

'I think you dropped this.' She blinked. In his hand he held a white orchid. 'It was in your hair earlier,' he reminded her softly.

'You've changed your clothes,' she said stupidly.

'I'm going somewhere,' he explained.

Her mind snapped back into gear. 'Going?' She gave a quick glance at the window. 'Oh! With Lisa?' She took in a huge breath. This was worse than she'd thought! 'Why, you——!'

He launched himself forwards and clamped his hand over her mouth. Tanya struggled furiously, jabbing her elbows into his chest and kicking at him with her bare heels. It hurt.

'Keep still, dammit, or I'll crush the breath out of you!' he muttered. When she took no notice, his powerful arm tightened around her ribs, making it impossible for her to do anything but snatch short, shallow breaths in and out of her nose.

Muttering something grim in Hungarian, he propelled her at double-quick speed along the terrace and to a more isolated back section of the house. All the while she was thinking miserably that István had been in Lisa's room. He'd done something terrible that had made Lisa cry, then had forced her to keep quiet while...

'Mmph!' she protested furiously.

'And "Mmph" to you,' he said irritably, pushing her against the wall and glaring at her.

I loathe you! her eyes told him silently, vehemently as the distressing heat of anger, despair and disgust coiled inside her, flowing through her veins till she felt ready to explode with an incandescent rage.

'Well, you're persistent, I'll say that for you,' he mused. 'If ever I need a bodyguard, I'll know where to come. What *did* you think you were doing?' His hand lifted a fraction, though not far enough for her to open her mouth wide and scream.

'I thought I was capturing a rapist,' she seethed, her lips softly bumping against the warm palm. She made a mental note to choose words that didn't cause her mouth to move much.

His eyebrows sped up in admiration. 'Brave of you,' he murmured silkily, then glanced at the stake. 'Was that before or after you went hunting for vampires?'

'Vampire! One only!' she corrected furiously. 'You!'

'I wonder what I've done to earn that description?' he mused, letting his hand drift over her mouth, then over her chin and around her jaw to her neck, where it hovered, his fingers lightly stroking her jugular vein. And she tilted her head back as far as she dared, trying to avoid the warm pressure of the heel of his hand. 'Granted I do my best work at night——'

'Vampires,' she muttered, 'suck people dry to feed their own needs. They leave them to bleed!' She warmed to the subject, driven to the heights of frustration by the amusement in his eyes. He had no *right* to find this situation funny! It was tragic! 'Vampires leave people half alive!' she jerked. 'There's a whole heap of corpses strewn behind you——'

'Good God, Tanya! You're lurching into melodrama,' he chided. 'This isn't a horror movie.'

'Isn't it?' she cried heatedly. 'Aren't you the arch-villain? You're a destroyer, István, an evil, amoral, uncaring brute! I never thought you'd stoop so low! I hate you,' she whispered vehemently. 'I wish to God that I'd driven the stake right into your evil heart!'

'Lighten up, Tan,' he said evenly. 'You're overreacting. Take a deep breath and——'

'Don't soothe me!' she grated. 'Is Lisa coming?'

He looked puzzled. 'Coming to what? Is there some party I'm missing—other than John's stag night?'

Exasperated beyond belief, she glared. 'Is she coming down the rope?' she ground out, laboriously spelling it out for him. 'Were you and she planning on going somewhere tonight?'

'I imagine that's a cautious way of asking if we're eloping,' he drawled. 'No. I was just visiting.'

'*Visiting*?' she cried incredulously.

'Why not? She is an old friend of the family,' he answered reasonably.

'Oh, all above board, was it? Then why leave by the emergency exit?' she asked sarcastically.

The corners of his mouth curved up, distracting her for a moment. 'Was I ever conventional?' he murmured.

'You can take that look of sweet-child innocence off your face!' she stormed. 'This is a bride we're talking about, on the eve of her wedding! It's not normal for a bride to receive visits from men. You made her cry!' she accused fiercely, half of her distress being for Lisa. The rest was despair for her shattered illusions. 'I *heard* her crying. What the devil did you do to her?' she wailed.

The black eyes glinted. 'Sank my teeth into her white neck and drew a pint or two of blood!' he growled. 'Is there much more of this? I can't stop long—I must get back before the sun rises. My grave's getting cold.'

'Carry on joking like that, and I'll help you into it!' she spluttered. 'You swine! What kind of state is Lisa in now? How can she marry John? Don't you care what a mess you make of people's lives?' she demanded hotly, her breast rising high with indignation beneath the simple white bodice.

'It cuts both ways,' he said curtly. 'You're making one hell of a mess of mine at the moment.' His eyes dropped to where her night-dark skin swelled above the thin cotton and suddenly she felt frighteningly defenceless. His hand rested now on her bronzed, bare shoulder and she could feel its heat right through the bone.

'I wish I were! I'd love to make you suffer!'

'All is possible,' he said quietly.

'You give me hope,' she said tightly. 'Now tell me what you did to make her cry.'

'Nothing!' he growled. 'Forget you saw me.'

'*Forget*?' she raged. 'How can I, in all conscience?'

'Because you must not wreck Lisa's marriage.'

Her mouth dropped open at his sheer effrontery. '*I* mustn't wreck it? What a nerve! Are you telling me that you've spent part of the night with her but still *want* her to get married?' she asked in disbelief.

'Of course.'

'Why? Because...?' One explanation. Her mute, pained eyes completed the sentence. Because tonight you might have made her pregnant. Dear God, she thought, trembling. He'd destroyed the three of them: John, Lisa and herself. For the thought of her friend actually in István's arms was unbearable and hurt her more than she could ever have imagined.

'Tanya,' he said softly. 'Let John remain in blissful ignorance——'

'Ignorance of what?' she asked in a low whisper, fist pressing hard against her lurching heart. 'The carefully calculated rape of his bride?'

István let out a sharp exhalation that steam-heated her sensitised skin. 'God give me patience! Just stop blathering on and listen to the sounds going on for a moment, will you?' he ordered.

Quivering uncontrollably, she did so. The stag party rumbled on in the background. She strained her ears and heard the breeze rustling the leaves of the beech wood beyond the lake, the snort of horses from a stable near by, the quick ebb and flow of István's breath. Nothing else. The night seemed to embrace them with secrecy.

'What am I supposed to hear?' she demanded hoarsely.

'Nothing unusual. That's the point. If I've raped Lisa, why isn't she screaming for the police? And don't leap into melodrama again and say I've probably beaten her up or gagged her or some other stupid remark.'

Tanya's eyes flashed at the caustic tone in his voice. 'You're implying that Lisa *willingly* consented to— to——'

'Sex?' he offered coldly.

'To...' The word still refused to pass her lips. 'To...to s——' She abandoned the attempt. He'd said it for her. 'I won't believe that!' she whispered. 'You must have forced her against her will——'

'We're completely excluding the possibility of a chat, then,' he said drily.

'Why go to all the trouble of shinning up and down a pair of knotted curtains if all you wanted was a chat?' she scathed. 'Haven't you heard that someone's invented the telephone?'

'You can't cuddle someone over the phone.'

Tanya flinched. Now they were getting somewhere. 'So you, the womanising champion of south-west England, felt in desperate need of a *cuddle*?'

'Not exactly,' he admitted, his mouth twitching. 'God, you're stubborn when you get something into your head! Now pay attention. When you were in your room, did you hear anything other than crying?' he asked quietly.

'No. Should I?' she scowled.

'I rest my case. You see, Tanya,' he drawled, 'when I make love to a woman, she doesn't stay silent. Nor, for that matter,' he added, while she grew steadily a brighter scarlet, 'do I.'

He gave that time to sink in and in her mind's eye she imagined him, huskily groaning, throwing his head back and crying out in pleasure. Disturbed by the highly sexual imagery, she drew her teeth over her lower lip.

'What are you saying?' she muttered.

'Of course Lisa invited me in herself,' he said patiently. 'I phoned her to talk and she asked me to come. I couldn't climb up to her room without her help, could I? She obviously had to take down the curtains and knot them and tie them to the bedpost.'

'But why bother to climb up to her room in the first place?' she demanded irritably.

'Because,' he said patiently, 'when I walked up the stairs, intending to call in on her, I saw that your door was open and you were sitting like some old battleaxe of a duenna, poised to throw valuable vases at any man who ventured near your appointed charge. You had a dreamy look in your eyes and a definitely glazed expression as if you were thinking of something rather pleasurable,' he smiled, 'but I knew you'd wake up and scream blue murder if I tried to creep up to Lisa's door.'

'So you persuaded her to let you in the window. You tricked her,' she said coldly. 'What then?'

'We had a chat.'

'All that effort for a chat?' she scathed.

'She needed me,' he said simply.

Something inside her snapped. '*You*? Why would she want a heart-to-heart with you and not me? Why, knowing your track record, should she trust you?'

'Tanya, does it matter why? She does. And I knew I could help. I have helped.'

'Don't kid yourself!' she said bitterly. 'Your "help", your "cuddles"——' She stopped. This was doing her no good at all. 'This might have been just one in a line of one-night stands for you,' she choked out, wishing she could crawl into a dark corner and howl like a wounded animal, 'but for Lisa——'

'No one must know,' István interrupted. 'And don't tell her you know, either. She'd be utterly appalled and ashamed to learn that you knew I'd been to see her tonight.'

Tanya stared at him helplessly, wondering, hoping that all they'd done was talk together. Was he right? Would Lisa rather keep this rendezvous a secret? She wavered. 'I can't believe she'd let you in!' she argued. 'She'd know that it would kill John if he found out that you'd been in his bride's bedroom the night before her wedding!'

'Tan, Lisa let me see her because she was——'

'Grateful?' She gulped, remembering that he'd claimed Lisa felt obligated. 'For the money you laid out on the reception?'

He frowned. 'If she was grateful it would be for the music scholarship in Budapest.'

'What,' asked Tanya, taut with tension, 'did you have to do with that?'

'I arranged it.'

She groaned. Another nail in Lisa's coffin! And in her letters during the past year Lisa had never even mentioned meeting István. Was that guilt? 'Why?' she asked shakily.

'Because I knew she was very talented and wasn't getting anywhere in Britain. That seemed a waste when I had friends in the academy I could introduce her to,' he explained.

'You...always encouraged her musical ability.' Tanya was beginning to see the picture. He'd kept a hold on Lisa by getting her the scholarship. No wonder she was grateful! 'We thought she'd won the place by talent alone——'

'She did, but first a few key people had to hear her play. That's how it goes, Tanya. If you don't walk into the wood, you don't find the trees. I'm all for giving fate a hefty nudge now and then.'

Brilliant, she'd say. Lisa had been party to her own fate. The opportunity to study in Budapest had been little more than a ploy. Nothing he ever did was for other people; it was always for himself.

'How long have you been demanding sexual favours as a payment?' she snapped.

'Don't be ridiculous! I don't demand,' he said tightly. 'I get offers.'

'I see.' She took a moment to consider this information. And of course it was true. István had that kind of effect on women, she thought morosely. He strolled about looking ravishing, they allowed themselves to *be* ravished. 'Then explain this. If she was that grateful and that crazy about you,' she reasoned, seeing a flaw in his version of events, 'why should she accept John's proposal of marriage?'

István smiled faintly and touched Tanya's sullen mouth with his forefinger. Its brief pressure made her flinch and sent a curl of hot anger into the pit of her stomach.

'I'm flattered you think I have the power to wipe out all competition,' he murmured silkily.

'I don't!' she retorted heatedly. 'But then I know what a rat you are. I can see that *some* women might think you're exciting and I'm the first to admit that John's not the most exciting guy in the world. He's decent, kind and conventional and the sort of guy a woman would marry when she wanted to settle down and start a family...' Her words tailed away at István's quick frown, his hastily lowered lashes. It was a year since Lisa had left England. Her pulses raced. Long enough. Her face drained of colour. 'Is—is she...pregnant already?' she faltered, resisting the overwhelming impulse to say 'again'.

He gave her a hard, cold stare. 'I beg your pardon?'

'You want Lisa to marry. She's unhappy...crying... Are—are you p-planning to foist your—your—bastard on my brother?' she croaked.

'My God!' he muttered tightly. 'That's a nasty little mind you've got in there.'

The hazel of her eyes was obliterated by tears as she thought of John's joy, his exuberance when he'd met her at the airport only a few hours ago. Piteously, she lifted her small oval face to István's icy black gaze. 'Tell me!' she pleaded. 'Is she pregnant?' And she waited in terror for his answer, knowing it might change all their lives.

István's expression was thunderous. Thickly, his voice barely audible, he muttered, 'Not as far as I know.'

'Oh, you're impossible!' she wailed. 'I can't stand this any longer! Let me go! I must see Lisa and get the whole story——'

'Damn you! Leave her alone! She's exhausted and she needs to sleep, or people will realise——'

'That she spent the night in her ex-lover's arms!' Tanya cried almost incoherently. 'Well, I'm going to tell John that I found you shinning down a rope from her room!'

István shifted closer in deliberate intimidation. 'For the last time,' he said with tight menace, 'I'm telling you to forget this! We chatted. No more.'

'I can't believe that,' she moaned, wanting to all the same.

'Well, you've got to!' he ordered. 'Let John marry the girl he's hankered after for years but never felt able to offer a future till now, and let his wedding-day go ahead as planned.'

It would be so easy. But... 'If I do that,' she cried wildly, 'you'll think you can slip into Lisa's bed any time you like!'

'Nice opinion you have of your friend's morals,' he said sarcastically. 'And mine. God, you make me angry, Tanya!'

He was just looking at her, nothing else. But even in the half-darkness that was enough to overwhelm her, to make her tongue thicken with fear. There was something devilish in the sharpness of his angular cheekbones, the softly sensual mouth, the dramatic intensity of his dark gaze.

She wondered nervously what he'd been doing these last four years. How much fast living he'd done, how many women he'd ruined and children he'd fathered in his careless disregard for the consequences of his intense sexual needs. More than his share, she decided, finding herself drowning in the black depths of his blazing eyes. And the pain scoured through her body, leaving her weak and virtually without defences.

'It's not Lisa's morals I blame,' she said miserably. 'It's yours. You know exactly what you're doing. All you've got to do is turn on the charm. Sometimes you don't even bother to do that. You merely put on that aloof, see-if-I-care expression and stand in a corner and scowl at women and they can't——'

'Help themselves?' he queried, his eyebrow arcing in weary contempt. 'Oh, come, Tanya! It's up to them whether they take up my sexual challenges or not. Usually they want a little excitement, a little danger, a brief flirtation with the unknown.'

'How dare you? That's insulting to women——' she began shakily.

'I have no illusions about the role they select for me,' he rasped. 'They're looking for a shot of adrenalin, straight into the bloodstream. I'm sexually creative, I don't fumble. I'm cheaper than sky-diving, less damaging than pure alcohol and provide more thrills and entertainment than a good video. Fun. Thrills, spills. That's what they want.'

'Is that what you offered Lisa?' she asked in horror. And she wrestled with the thought that, having known István's lovemaking once before, Lisa might have hankered for one repeated night of pure, unbridled wickedness in view of marriage to dear, steady John. Oh, God, she moaned silently, I'm crucifying myself with this knowledge!

'Human nature is full of mysteries. Women see me as attractive because they think I'm the bad guy,' he growled.

'Well, I despise you for trading on it,' she grated.

He lifted his shoulders dismissively. 'Do I?'

'Did you or did you not make love to Lisa?' she demanded. 'You must tell me, or——' His fingers dug into her shoulder muscle, silencing her as she stubbornly struggled not to cry out.

'There is no "or", Tanya,' he said menacingly. 'Forget that you ever saw me come from Lisa's room, for the sake of her future.'

She whimpered in her throat and his grip mercifully eased. 'Do you care for her?' she whispered. He nodded and she winced. That was worse. A caring István would be irresistible to any woman. 'This is awful,' she moaned. 'So do I. I love Lisa dearly and I don't want to hurt her,' she said in a low tone.

'Then let her marry John!' he growled in exasperation.

'You don't know what you're asking!' she cried piteously. 'I'm just from a small village and I don't have your sophistication or your more unconventional morals. I believe that marriage is forever, that you love someone and respect them and build on that love till the day you die. That's what I want for me and for everyone I love. However fond I am of Lisa, if she intends to play false to John, then I can't turn a blind eye and...' She took a deep, painful breath. 'He's my brother. I care for him and I care for truth and morality. My first loyalty is to him, to all the values I believe in! I can't let John marry Lisa with this on my conscience,' she said angrily. 'Do you think I want to tell him? Do you think it's going to be easy? But I have to!'

'Duty!' he growled.

'You won't know of such things,' she muttered, 'but yes, I feel a sense of moral obligation to my brother. I wish I had the ability to hurt you as you've hurt us! One of these days——'

He pulled her roughly against him in temper. She reached up to push his shoulders and met resisting muscle so hard and tensed that she panicked. First she tried to slide one way and then the other, but the movement of her thinly clad body against the soft linen of his shirt and the intimacy of his thighs merely brought an irritated exhalation of breath from him. And somehow their physical contact produced a quiver in her that radiated from her loins and continued to flow in limb-weakening stabs through the length and breadth of her body.

He looked down, his eyes glinting with an intense passion. 'I won't be threatened by you,' he said in soft savagery. 'And I will *not* allow you to ruin Lisa's wedding.'

'Why are you so determined it must go ahead,' she cried in bewilderment, 'when you claim that you and she are l-l...?'

'Say it,' he snarled. 'Why do the words stick in your throat, Tanya? Why don't you like to think of me with a woman?'

'Because...'

'Yes?' he murmured huskily.

She shook her head to release the paralysis that was creeping over her brain and her tawny hair tumbled about her face and shoulders, prompting István to toy with it, his fingers torturing her, touching her bare flesh and making her almost hysterical.

'Because I fear for her happiness, for John's, and mine!' She threw her head back and groaned. 'Oh, why do you always make me so unhappy?' She felt the tears welling up. He didn't know what deep emotions were like, what pain was, and she wanted to hurt him as she'd been hurt. 'You split our family in two. You destroyed it! God, István, you've hurt everyone I've ever loved!' she sobbed. 'Father's never been the same since Mother died. He loved her so much——'

István's face was stony. 'We all did, dammit!'

She paused, stopped in her tracks by the hoarse whisper. For the first time, through a curtain of tears, she saw behind István's carefully applied mask and through to the desolation that lay behind his guarded eyes. Quiet though his voice had been, he was shaken—actually grief-stricken. He'd loved her mother, then! she thought in surprise.

'I never knew. You never showed it.' She saw him swallow and realised he was moved.

'No.'

She hesitated, daunted by his pinched expression, remembering he'd been taught not to reveal emotion. And wondered why he was doing so now. 'I—— If only you'd sent a letter when you left, some explanation——'

'I sent a letter. I imagine your father tore it up,' he said in clipped tones. 'It was understandable, I suppose. He thought I'd been ungrateful for the sacrifices he'd made. I sent another letter when Ester died.' He cleared the hoarseness that had crept into his throat. 'I hoped he might ring to say it would be all right if I came to the funeral. I didn't want to arrive uninvited and turn the occasion into a slanging match. It was bad enough that she'd died so tragically without me causing more anguish.'

'I thought—I thought you didn't care,' she said in a forlorn voice and she wondered if Lisa had known of his wounded feelings, since she and István had been so close; whether Lisa understood his love for his foster mother and respected his decision to save the family from more pain. She remembered with a lurch of her heart that Lisa had said something about István being misunderstood. 'It's not like Father to bear a grudge,' she whispered.

'He resented me,' replied István curtly. 'As a Christian, he was appalled to feel that way. He despised himself for being jealous. It was an emotion he couldn't control and it made things worse between us.'

'Poor Father,' she said huskily. 'Poor Mother, caught between you two.'

'I wish to God I could have come to her funeral,' said István in a soft growl. He turned his head a little, presenting his hard profile as he listened. And she too could hear the stag party breaking up at last. 'Come on,' he snapped.

'What——?'

To her fury, he'd pressed his hand over her mouth again. 'I can't trust you,' he explained grimly. 'You're not malleable enough yet. You're still entertaining stupid notions of stopping Lisa's wedding and I won't let you do that. Somehow, Tanya, in one way or another, I must guarantee your silence.'

CHAPTER SIX

BEFORE his words could even sink in, István had whipped Tanya around and was forcing her rapidly across the terrace, her bare feet hardly touching the ground. Resisting everything he did, she made herself as heavy as she could, but István gave an impatient grunt and lifted her higher, hugging her to his body so that her spine curved into his chest and loins while her legs dangled uselessly in the air.

They negotiated the curving steps to the lawn and her body was bumped ignominiously against his. She became aware with an acute sense of embarrassment that a hard ridge of heat was pressing against the cleft between her small buttocks.

Her high whine of sheer panic filtered through the gaps between his fingers, provoking an outrush of his warm breath on to the side of her face. She felt his strong arm beneath her knees, the transferral of her weight, and then she was curled up in his arms and staring nervously at his set face while he loped across the lawn with long, easy strides.

It was several moments before she realised that her mouth was free and that she could scream if she wanted to. By then, however, he'd reached the stable block, unlatched a door and shut it behind him with a flick of his heel. She smelt the warm, welcomingly familiar aroma of hay and horses and then he'd switched on a light to reveal a double row of stalls occupied by tethered horses, snorting and complaining at the intrusion.

And something stopped her from speaking: the astonishing beat of István's heart, faster than it should be, hammering like the thunder of hooves in her ear. Perhaps he wasn't as fit as he looked, she thought. Or... She gulped, remembering his arousal.

'What—what are you going to do?' she whispered.

'Persuade you to co-operate.' With a cruel lack of haste, he slowly slid her down the hard length of his too male body and something—fear, perhaps—made her dizzy.

She swayed and grabbed his arm. 'István!' she croaked.

'I've got you,' he said huskily, catching her around the waist.

Her eyes flicked up rebelliously at the wealth of meaning in his words. Assuming a cold hauteur, she picked off his fingers one by one, confused at the effort it took and how much amusement her intense concentration afforded him.

'Don't be too sure of that! Short of slitting my tongue, you can't stop me from seeing Lisa and demanding an explanation,' she said shakily. 'Nor can you stop me from letting my brother know what you've done!'

'True,' he admitted. 'That's why I need a little time to work on you, to persuade you,' he elaborated, seeing her horrified expression.

'But—it's the middle of the night!' she wailed.

'Can you sleep? *Could* you sleep now?' he asked.

'No,' she said sullenly. 'But how do you think you're going to persuade me?'

'Would you like me to make love to you?' he queried, his mouth curling with a sensuality that mesmerised her.

To her dismay, desire darkened her eyes. She could feel her body melting at the thought and could do nothing to stop it. Yes. Very much. 'No!' she replied hoarsely, despairing at her need for a man who treated women with such profound contempt. There was nothing to explain her feelings. Other than madness. 'How you can suggest that I'd want you, after everything you've done to Lisa, both now and in the past, how you managed to slip into her room tonight—of all nights——'

'Is that a no?' he enquired drily.

She shook with rage. 'You—you——! Ohhh! You're impossible! You're impervious to everything—entreaties, insults, normal laws of decency——'

'Patience,' he soothed. 'We haven't begun. Hold your judgement a while.'

There was a warm, affectionate tone to his voice and it unsettled her. 'Begun what?' she asked warily.

The warmth deepened.

A liquid light had come into his eyes that was melting her again and Tanya couldn't fathom why her mouth felt dry. She licked her lips and saw his eyes follow the movement, her tongue halting partway through its journey.

'A gentle revelation, the slow dance where the remaining veils are gradually lifted, one by one, until finally everything is disclosed. There's no other way to do this.'

'István...' she croaked.

'Come and meet destiny,' he said quietly, reaching for her limp hand.

Her pulses began to race, warning her of danger. She knew now the pull of the inexplicable; the surge of exhilaration in her bloodstream as she contemplated accepting his challenge, reckless though that would be. 'I'm not going anywhere with you,' she said grimly.

'Look at the facts, Tanya,' he said quietly. 'I am much stronger than you. I could force you to do whatever I wanted. You noticed I was aroused. This is as good a place to take you as any. But you will have also noticed that I'm not making love to you, I haven't ripped your dress off, tempting though the idea is, and you're not currently in danger of sharing a stall with a Lippizaner stallion, a pile of straw and me.'

'Please be reasonable! You have to let me go!' she muttered.

'I can't allow that. At the moment you're a liability so you have to come with me. I'll give you a choice: come willingly, or be dragged, because you can be certain

that come you will,' he said, his voice hardening. 'We've
got a lot to talk about; I need time for that and somewhere warm to get you comfortable so you can listen
and be persuaded. Then I imagine you'll want to catch
a few hours' sleep before you have to dress for the
wedding.' He tipped his head on one side enquiringly.
'What's it to be?' he rapped out at her. 'Rough and ready
or dainty and dignified?'

'Of course I'm not going anywhere with you! I don't
trust you,' she cried stubbornly.

'I don't exactly trust you either,' he said sardonically.

Her heart sank. Logic might tell her all kinds of things,
but she knew from past experience that István was
lawless. He disregarded barriers, acknowledged no limits.
And he'd do anything to get his own way. Anything. She
shuddered. His thumb was idly caressing the erratic pulse
in her wrist, sending it haywire.

'I'd be crazy to go with you,' she said, her voice
irritatingly thick. 'I want to go back. Take me back,'
she begged.

'Scared?' he teased.

She flushed. 'Yes.'

'It's not far. The happiness of several people rests on
your decision,' he pointed out quietly. 'I want to talk
you round to my way of thinking. All you have to do is
listen.'

Her eyes flipped up to his. 'And then——?' The
tremble of her lip and the fear in her eyes completed her
sentence.

'I'm a sensualist. For me there would be no joy in
raping a woman,' he growled, his eyes holding hers with
a mesmeric ferocity.

A long gasp of relief fled from her tense body. That
made sense, at least. But he could talk to her here. She'd
listen to whatever he had to say and make up her own
mind. If he made any overtures, thinking he could persuade her that way, she could always take the first opportunity to run like mad.

'You've got half an hour,' she said coldly. 'We talk here.'

'That'll be long enough.' His eyes narrowed at the pleased look on her face. 'But not here. I insist on that. And by the way, *if* you try to get away and warn John, I'll go straight to Lisa and abduct her.' She glared and looked guilty and he roared with laughter, making her heart reluctantly turn somersaults. Oh, glory, she groaned. He was so ruinously handsome! 'I could see your brain working,' he said wryly. 'Let's go. Can't keep destiny waiting.'

'I'm hardly likely to find it in a stable,' she said crossly.

'No?' He drew her gently down the line of horses and lifted her chin with an unfairly tender forefinger. 'Wrong again. Meet Destiny.'

She swallowed, the lurch in her stomach indicating that she must be afraid. Her confused eyes focused on the gorgeous creature he indicated, black, sleek . . .

'A horse?' she exclaimed in surprise, ogling the lines of the impatient stallion's magnificent body.

'Expecting something else?'

She ignored him and went to stroke Destiny's nose and snuffle a welcome. 'Hello, Destiny,' she said softly. 'You're gorgeous! Is he a Lippizaner?' The Hungarian breed had a reputation of being mettlesome and lively—quite difficult to handle—but this one was a sweetie. Oh, the joy of riding an animal like that! The thrill of a fast gobbling-up of the ground, the wind in her hair——

He laughed softly. Dazed—dazzled even—she wondered what had happened to lift his mood so dramatically. 'Lift up your skirt,' he murmured huskily, taking a blanket from where it hung over the side of the stall.

She froze. Eyed the blanket. Then turned slowly, her eyes transfixed by the softness of his expression. Contemplating pleasure! she thought grimly. 'A stall, some hay and thou?' she said icily, reinterpreting Omar Khayyám's love poem. And when he laughed again in delight, she felt so furious with him that she brought the full weight of her hand across his face, whipping his head sideways with the force.

He did nothing. His skin, however, turned white, then pink, and before her horrified, mortified eyes the imprint of her hand fired like a rosy brand on the darkness of his cheek.

'Now I've had enough. Get up there,' he said tersely, indicating the horse, and threw the blanket over the stallion's back.

A blaze of his black eyes stopped the hot protest on her lips. He was seriously angry. But she'd hesitated too long. Boldly he reached down and caught the hem of her skirt in his hands, yanking it roughly up to her thighs.

Appalled, she stared at her bare legs, his hands still lingering intimately on her quivering skin. 'You *brute*!' she whispered, close to tears.

'Yes,' he agreed softly. 'Now *get up*!'

He wasn't in a mood to take any refusal. He'd throw her up there if she hesitated. Trembling, she held her skirts high while he linked his hands, lifted one leg and placed her small foot in his open palm then vaulted on to the horse's back. No saddle. He was used to that; she wasn't.

'Where...?' She gulped. 'How far——?'

'Just shut up,' he said curtly.

Grim-faced, he slipped a bridle over Destiny's head and led him out of the stable, leaping up lightly with the ease of a circus-rider behind her. 'Of all the women I've ever known,' he growled in her ear, 'you've given me the most trouble.'

'Good!' she muttered.

At a kick of his heels, the horse sprang into life. It clattered over the cobbles in the yard and then was thudding over the turf towards the wood.

'Hang on.'

She hung. They bent low in the saddle, their two bodies as one, the speed, the excitement of the mad dash through the wood and beyond filling Tanya with an inexplicable joy.

His body warmed hers, his arms enclosed her safely and the thrill of that wild ride sparked every nerve she possessed into glorious life. There was just the rhythmical sound of hooves flashing over the ground and the stallion's steady, snorting breath that vaporised in the cool night air, but those sounds were well-loved ones for Tanya and riding was one of her great pleasures.

For the duration of that ride she forgot her troubles and revelled in the effervescing of her blood in her veins and the sheer exhilaration of being so intensely alive.

'Enjoying it?' he yelled in her ear.

Wonderful. But she wouldn't tell him of the freedom in her heart and the merciful respite from her problems. He laid his cheek against hers and a fierce ripple raced through her from head to toe. Her thigh muscles contracted.

'On, Destiny!' she urged under her breath.

István's powerful arms commanded both her and the stallion, his sharp eyes and quick reflexes keeping them out of trouble as his deft and gentle hands steered them over the moonlit ground unerringly. He was a born rider, she marvelled in awe. He and the horse were in total harmony and for a brief time she became part of that unity.

'You love it,' he murmured. 'You always have, you always will. You and I, riding hard and shedding all the trappings of duty and responsibility that normally contain us.'

She snorted. He knew nothing of duty or responsibility.

'There it is. Up there.'

István used all his skill as a horseman to reduce the headlong gallop to a more sedate canter because the capricious stallion so obviously wanted to go on forever. Ahead, she saw a small building, long and low, its whitewashed walls gleaming in the darkness. As they came closer, she saw that the cottage was thatched, with a wooden loggia running the whole length of the building.

When they were a few yards away, he slid from the horse's back and looped the reins over the post of a sweep-pole well, the shadowy hint of a smile hovering about his lips as he looked up at her. 'Excited?' he asked huskily.

It was a reasonable assumption. Without realising it, she'd been laughing. Her eyes were sparkling and she was pink-cheeked from the ride. Every inch of her tingled as though she were sickening for a fever. Excited? she thought in amazement. And how!

But her throat constricted at the smouldering—what was it? The den of wild things in his eyes. He was going to ensure her silence. A little scared, and contrary to all she'd learnt, she chose to avoid his waiting arms and fling one long, smooth leg over the stallion's head to slither down the wrong side, landing in an ungainly heap on the ground.

'*That* excited!' marvelled István sarcastically, calming his irritated horse.

She marched stiff-backed towards the cottage, wriggling her dress down haughtily as she went. He caught her up and pushed open the plank door. It opened to a small room dominated by a beehive-shaped construction which she imagined must be a clay oven. To her surprise, it was alight, the glow warm and welcoming.

'Yours?' she asked, intrigued, turning warily to István. He ducked under the low lintel and her fascinated gaze lingered on the thatch which was at least three feet thick.

'I'll light the lamps.'

He disappeared into a room that led off to the left. The oil lamp and candles flickered into life and spilled their warm gleam everywhere. Her face softened with pleasure, though she stayed by the door. Only women intent on sexual suicide would go into a bedroom with István.

'It's warm,' she said, drawn to the cosy room.

'You can't beat thick walls, thatch roofs and tile stoves for keeping out the cold,' he remarked, indicating a monster stove that stood taller than him. He tentatively patted the surface of its green glazed tiles and she had the impression that it was hot.

'Someone's kept the stove in. And who lit that oven? You?' Her keen eyes scanned the room in more detail, moving on hastily from the canopied beds against the wall. It didn't seem his kind of house. 'And who made that jam——?'

'I'm renting the place,' he answered smoothly.

'Jam?' she cried in disbelief. 'You spend your evenings making *jam*?'

István's mouth twitched and then came under control. 'Bit of a quantum leap, that one, isn't it?' he acknowledged. 'Sit down. We're not here to discuss my leisure activities.'

'I'd rather we went into the living room,' she said cautiously.

'This is it.' He rose and indicated a table and, beneath it, a bench. 'The clean room. Bed or board. Choose,' he said on his way out. 'I'll heave some more logs into the oven. It feeds the stove. Excuse me.'

The bench wobbled when she sat on it. Feeling rather like Goldilocks trying furniture out for size, she decided she needed something to cradle her tired body and eyed the beds with their big, fat duvets enviously. She compromised and leaned against one, waiting warily for István, all her nerves jangling.

The room puzzled her. Something was wrong in it. Outside it had looked like one of the traditional Hungarian houses she'd occasionally seen on the way from the airport: timber-framed with adobe walls and a steep roof with snow-guards. A peasant's house, as István had claimed, and certainly there were strings of paprika drying in festive swags from a dresser and pretty embroidered cloths on the back of the chairs.

But, other than that, the furnishings and furniture told another tale. Already her fingers had detected that the bedding was of fine linen, silk and gold-thread embroidery, each piece marked with the same crest as the one that had been carved into the headboard. A family crest, she thought, intrigued. A two-headed eagle, flowers, corn...

Alert, she sat up more erect. Peasants didn't have family portraits in oils, dainty porcelain arranged on satinwood dressers and silver-framed photographs——

'Photos!' she breathed, heading straight for them.

He got there before she did. 'Private,' he said abruptly, blocking her way. With a swift movement, he recklessly swept the silver frames flat on their faces.

'You're hiding something,' she accused.

'Some *things*,' he corrected smoothly. 'Now. Lisa——'

'There's lipstick on your face!' she accused sharply, as the lamplight lit the side of his head.

His fingers went immediately to the stain on his cheekbone. 'Blood?' he suggested wickedly.

She scowled. 'Mouth-shaped?'

He grimaced. 'You're going to be hard work, aren't you?'

She was wasting time. He was as guilty as hell. 'No,' she snapped, her misery deeper than ever. She was living a nightmare. He'd made love to Lisa. 'I'm leaving,' she whispered jerkily. 'I've decided I'm going to tell John——'

'Know the way, do you?' he drawled.

Aghast, she whirled on her heel. 'I...' Frantically she tried to recall which direction they'd taken on the twisting journey. It had been dark; István and Destiny had known the way but she'd never find her way back. 'I'd follow the path.' She waited for his reaction to this.

'Which one would that be? The one to the marshes, the one deeper into the forest——?' He leaned forwards confidingly. 'I'd better warn you about the wild boars. They're more dangerous than the wolves, some people believe,' he said helpfully.

Her eyes closed in brief despair. 'So I need you to take me back.'

'You certainly do,' he agreed, a triumphant light in his mocking eyes. 'And if you don't agree to let John

and Lisa marry as if nothing happened tonight, then...'
His chest expanded in an extravagant sigh and she felt
all the hackles on the back of her neck rise up.

'Then?' she prompted, warily.

He smiled. 'Then I must keep you here until the
wedding is over.'

He was exhausting, she thought wearily; never giving
up, never letting go, like some ruthless wolf, biting and
snarling at everything that challenged him until he had
established his position in the pack.

'Let me go back. I'm tired,' she said dully.

'Tough. I'm in deadly earnest, Tanya.'

The gas hissed gently. The air began to thicken as they
stared at one another, the pulses in Tanya's throat beating
with a heavy laziness as if her blood was tired too.

'Then give me a good reason to say nothing,' she said
listlessly. The bed looked inviting. If only she could curl
up in it! 'But if you touch me, I swear I'll scream so
loud it'll burst your eardrums.'

'Lisa is my priority at the moment,' he said quietly
and she flinched. A gleam came into his eyes. 'You, I
can wait for.'

'Don't hold your breath,' she muttered.

Smiling to himself, István collected a bottle and two
glasses from a shelf and poured out thick red wine. Tanya
accepted one of the wafer-thin glasses, hoping the alcohol would revive her flagging spirits. Settling himself
on the edge of the table, his legs casually swinging, he
took a draught of the wine before turning his level gaze
on to her.

'Lisa's behaviour hasn't come as a surprise to me,' he
began quietly. 'She's been increasingly worried about her
marriage.'

Tanya's eyes widened. 'So I gathered,' she said
miserably. More secrets. Oh, dear heaven! she groaned
inside. She must get back and tell John! 'Let me go,'
she implored István in a trembling voice. 'Let's end
this charade!'

'You have to listen,' he growled. 'I'll make you listen if I have to tie you to the bed!'

'Oh, go on!' she moaned, waving a vague, tired hand. Nothing he said would make any difference. She knew what she had to do.

'Thanks,' he said sarcastically. 'I was going to. Unfortunately Lisa hasn't been able to talk about her worries recently, because I've been away for some time——'

'She has John!' frowned Tanya, annoyed at his assumption that he was the only person Lisa would turn to. 'If she was worried about their relationship, that's who she should have been talking to! Failing that, I'm at the end of a phone, or the postal system, and surely she has friends who are more qualified to talk about emotions than *you*!'

István's mouth tightened. 'This was something she couldn't talk to you about, or anyone else. Only me.'

'I see,' she said dully. She lifted her forlorn face. 'She must love you very much.'

'Oh, you little fool,' he told her softly as she fought back the tears, knowing she was a worse fool than he ever imagined. 'There are many kinds of love. Lisa is closer to me as a sister than you ever were.'

'You don't make love to sisters.' Sullenly Tanya reached out and placed her glass on the table. Her hand was shaking too much to hold it steady any longer.

'No,' he husked, capturing her fingers in his. 'You don't. *Csókolom.*' His head bent, he kissed her hand tenderly and then turned it over to touch his lips to the sensitive hollow in her palm.

Hastily Tanya snatched her hand away and retreated to the bed. 'What's she been worried about?' she asked hoarsely.

István took a sip of wine and then spoke more huskily. 'She's scared of two things in particular. One is that she might not be able to have children.'

'No!' she gasped in dismay. 'Poor darling...that's terrible... She never breathed a word. Why?' she wailed. 'She's my friend!'

'She was afraid you'd tell John,' he explained gently. 'She didn't want him to know because she's afraid to reveal the cause; that she'd lost her child four years ago.'

'Your child,' whispered Tanya through stiff lips. She dropped her gaze to conceal her anguish. How tragic, she thought sadly. The night before Lisa's wedding and she was racked with indecision. It was too cruel. Tanya's eyes were filled with misery when she could finally face István's glittering eyes again. 'I hope you realise that your past actions have caused problems all down the line,' she said bitterly.

He didn't answer but his expression hardened. 'Shall we stick to the problem and skip the recriminations?' he suggested coldly.

She didn't care if her words hurt him. Lisa was upset and on the brink of doing something stupid and it was all István's fault. 'You cold-blooded brute!' she muttered, giving vent to her feelings. But he was right. The problem of Lisa came first. He could wait. 'Is this a doctor's opinion, or hers?' she asked in clipped tones.

'A bit of both. The gynaecologist she spoke to after she lost the baby told her to be prepared for the possibility that she might not be able to have children. You see the problem. She's been agonising whether to tell John the *whole* story—— '

'That you got her pregnant!' she blurted out, her mouth bitter. 'You see what damage you've done! I can't ever have respect for a man who can't control his sexuality, whose first thought is his own pleasure, not the protection of an innocent woman!' she blazed.

'That's what I thought.'

'Behaviour like that shows a weak character,' she stormed.

'Yes,' he said gently. 'I'm afraid it does.'

She was astonished that he should agree with her and gaped at him in confusion. Her brain seemed to be putting up 'Closed for business' signs. 'Why are you eating humble pie?' she muttered.

'Even the most steadfast, reliable, conventional people have faults,' he remarked enigmatically. 'Nobody is a saint. You will think too highly of people you love. Don't be blind to their flaws.'

'If you're excusing what you did by suggesting John's probably as bad as you——!' she began heatedly.

'We all have feet of clay over *something*. An Achilles' heel. That——' He stopped, as though selecting his words with great care. 'That weakness has made Lisa think twice.'

'About running away with you?' Tanya mumbled.

'About marriage, about telling John anything at all.'

'You're not making sense,' she said irritably.

'I'm making more sense than you realise,' he said, pushing a tired hand through his hair. 'You'll know everything after the wedding.'

'Why not now?' she asked in a hard tone.

'Because I can't trust you to keep your mouth shut. I want to get some sleep, Tanya,' he said quietly. 'Can we sort this out first? You need to know what's been decided. Lisa's been chewing over her choices: to say nothing, to make a full confession, or to tell John that there's a risk she can't have children, without giving any specific reason.'

'John badly wants a family,' said Tanya, her eyes troubled.

'I know. That adds to the problem. That's what we were talking over; that's why she was crying. It's a dilemma she's tried to solve and which has torn her in two. I knew what was disturbing her and that I might be able to help. She didn't want you to know I was there, because you'd get the wrong idea. Which you did,' he pointed out.

'What did you advise her to do?' asked Tanya wearily.

'I don't give advice,' he said quietly. 'I get people to make up their own minds by asking them questions and making sure they know all the angles. I lead them along the road they really want to take, but perhaps don't dare. What I would do in her case, or even what I would like her to do if I were John, is irrelevant. Lisa has different needs, different feelings from me.'

To her surprise, he'd sounded infinitely wise and understanding. But then he'd been seriously involved in this. Tanya's tiredness swept over her and the loneliness in her heart deepened.

'What has she decided?' she frowned.

'To rely on the fact that John loves her, and that he'll continue to love her whether she can have children or not,' he answered, his narrowed eyes assessing her reaction. 'It's her decision and we must respect that, whatever our own feelings. I hope you'll now agree to let them get on with their lives without any interference.'

'I'm not sure,' she said slowly. 'I still can't understand your relationship with her——'

'Platonic. We talked,' he insisted.

It might be true. On the other hand... 'I think you're still a threat to John's happiness. Do you—do you still find Lisa attractive?' she asked tremulously.

'I've always found her attractive,' he smiled. Tanya bit her lip and glared at the amusement in his eyes. 'And my relationship with her is special. But I don't love her as John does and what she feels for me isn't love either.'

If not love, then perhaps it was passion that he felt. Or obsession, thought Tanya, unable to endure much more. The revelations were tearing her apart. 'You said she was scared of *two* things,' she reminded him listlessly, shifting her weight against the bed.

'Why don't you sit down?' he husked in a kind, caring tone. Presumably he caught the look of caution in her eyes, because he sighed and said, 'I'm not going to leap over and rip your dress off just because you're sitting on a bed,' failing to keep the amusement out of his voice. 'I told you before, if I want a woman it doesn't matter where she is. As far as I'm concerned, you'd be fine, just where you are. I'd make love to you anywhere; standing up, sitting down——' He grinned at her shocked

expression. 'The fight's going out of you; that's a sure
indication you're tired! Rest on the bed if you want while
we get this matter cleared up and we can both catch a
few hours' sleep.'

Her hands were already feeling the cosy softness of
the big, puffy duvet. It *was* tempting; she was tired . . .
It would be a kind of test. She paused uncertainly, her
hands braced on the bed. Then in an easy movement she
swung herself up and around, curling up with pleasure
on the comfortable mattress and arranging the plump
cushions behind her.

If he tried anything, she'd know for sure that he was
never, ever to be trusted. And she sat there full of tension,
because she was aware that she was probably too tired
and in need of affection to deny István a kiss. Which
would be tantamount to an open invitation . . . The
muscles in her body knotted with fear. Soon, very soon,
for her own safety, she *had* to persuade him to take her
back.

'You've got a few minutes only and then we really
must stop,' she said, prim-lipped.

'You sound like Miss Lattimer,' he smiled.

'Our village schoolteacher?' She nodded, smiling
faintly at the memory. 'I suppose I did.'

'In fact,' mused István, 'those were her exact words
that day I persuaded her to let the infants have rides on
my pony.'

'You were playing truant,' she said, and her smile
became warm as she remembered her classmates' excitement and her own pride that this generous benefactor was her brother.

'Pity she went off to check with the head of my prep
school to see if I was supposed to be home.'

Tanya sighed, remembering how angry Miss Lattimer
had been. 'She bawled you out and half the infants
howled because they never had a ride at all! It was as if
they'd seen paradise and been denied it.'

'Do you think it would have been better if I'd never
made the offer?' he asked gently. 'Would you say it's

better if people never glimpse paradise, but stay ignorant—but unscathed—for the whole of their lives?'

'That's your philosophy, isn't it?' she mused shrewdly. 'Head for paradise, whatever the cost, even if you fail to get there.'

'It's always worth a try, Tanya,' he said softly.

She gave a slight shrug of her shoulders. 'I don't know what's best. Some of those infants were awfully angry! What you said earlier, I suppose: that everyone has to make their own decision according to their character and needs. You, for instance, would never be happy doing anything ordinary. You've always hungered for danger and adventure. I'm——'

'Unfulfilled.'

Her body became tense and alert. He hadn't moved, but there was a tenderness in his eyes that rocked her. The gentle light from the lamp deepened the raven hues in his hair and painted his forehead and jutting cheekbones a gleaming gold. As she stared, the pupils of his eyes were melting into hers, the bow of his upper lip arching more sensually... and his lips parted with the increased rate of his breathing, his teeth showing a glistening whiteness. And she felt the prickles of fear lift the hairs on the back of her neck.

'How did we get on to this? We were discussing Lisa,' she said hoarsely.

'I got diverted. You'll respect her decision and say nothing, won't you?' he coaxed.

'I suppose so.' His beaming smile warmed her heart. She gulped nervously and tucked her feet under her so that she was ready to spring up if he moved a muscle. But he didn't, although the gap between them seemed to be already bridged by her terrible desire for him. It wouldn't take much for István to rein her in across that bridge. She could feel the control he had over her, as though she were a fresh, untrained colt and he the ultimate master with the whip hand, the sureness of touch, the ability to understand how to train an unbroken animal.

A horse was stronger than a man. Yet a man had the greater intelligence, the skill, the knowledge, to dominate. He'd broken in more horses than she could imagine. And perhaps women, too? *Her*?

She trembled.

'Are you cold?' he asked softly.

She shook her head, dumb with misery. 'Tired,' she said thickly. 'Very, very tired.'

'Of course,' he soothed in a husky growl. 'You must have had an early start this morning. Then there was the shock of finding out that I wasn't your brother, and it's been a long, endless night, hasn't it? Shall I take you back to the castle?'

'Mmm,' she agreed half-heartedly. In truth, she'd prefer to collapse here, on this lovely bed, rather than face the ride back. 'If you would.' Her exhausted brain registered that something was unfinished and she remained against the pillows, her brow furrowed as she struggled to remember what it was.

'Come on.' István rose in a purposeful way.

'Wait a minute!' Tanya frowned at him. 'I knew we weren't finished! I want to know the second thing Lisa was worried about.'

He scowled and looked at her from under his lowered brows. 'I don't think——'

'Everything,' she said, trying to rouse herself from her stupor. 'Tell me everything, or I'll insist that John knows.'

István sighed heavily. 'Dammit! You're irritatingly stubborn! OK. Though I dislike betraying a confidence.' He began to pace around the room and Tanya relaxed, the weariness spreading over her limbs. 'It's connected with what we've been discussing: that people think and behave very differently. You see, Lisa has been questioning her love for John.'

Tanya licked her dry lips. 'Because?' she faltered.

'She says she loves him, that of all men he's the one she wants to grow old with, but——'

'I knew it! I was afraid of this! She doesn't feel the passion she felt—perhaps *feels*—for you?' finished Tanya hoarsely.

This was dreadful, she thought unhappily. What should she do now? Let Lisa live a safe and contented life with John, or tell her to exorcise the ghost of István first—if that were possible? She groaned. *She'd* never managed to clear him from her mind; why should Lisa?

'It's not *quite* that. She's...' He hesitated, choosing his words carefully again, still pacing around the room as he used to when he'd spent too long inactive and needed to release his explosive energy. 'She's seen great passion. She knows what it's like, how it tears and hurts and fills someone so relentlessly that they can think of nothing else, do nothing else, plan for nothing else but its satisfaction.' His eyes turned full on her, burning into her as they'd never done before. 'Do you know what I'm talking about, Tanya? Am I ringing any bells in there?'

Her eyes were enormous pools of liquid green. István's ardent words had struck home. Of course she knew! She felt that passion. Her heart was leaping in her breast, shouting to be let out, her breath had moved to her throat and seemed to be attempting an escape bid from her body. There wasn't room, she thought in panic, for anything inside her other than the overwhelming, overpowering need she had for István.

'As you said,' she croaked, 'we're all different. For some people there can be passion without love.' He and Lisa. How that knowledge hurt! She tried to clear her throat without success. 'Excuse me,' she mumbled, apologising for her croak and massaging her neck gently. 'It's tiredness.'

'Passion without love. I see.'

Her eyes went to him like a homing pigeon. His back was to her and he was pouring out more wine for himself, his shoulders hunched over as he bent to the table. It couldn't be so, but he seemed sad and she remembered bitterly how desperate she'd been in their childhood to make him happy, to change that sorrow he bore like a burden. But now she wanted to offer...

Her breath drew in sharply at the unnerving discovery. Love.

That was her dearest wish. She wanted to give him her love and to be loved by him in return. It welled up inside her with the pain and threatening tears till she felt it might burst her open like a chestnut exploding in a fire. There was a love inside her so huge that she'd never known existed. And, judging by the sensations she was feeling now, her capricious, crazy heart seemed hell-bent on going against all wisdom and offering every ounce of her precious love to a man who wasn't fit to kiss her feet.

Slowly, while he continued to drink, unaware of the drama and tragedy being played out inside her, she lay back against the pillows and ruthlessly crushed that love. It could never be killed because it went too deep. It could be suppressed, however. The effort left her more exhausted than ever.

It was very quiet. The candles flickered. The warmth and tiredness embraced her and with no movement or sound from István, she finally fell into a deep, impenetrable sleep.

'Tanya! Tanya!'

An urgent voice woke her—that and the warm hand gently rocking her shoulder. 'What?' she mumbled reluctantly, her glued-up eyes refusing to open.

'Wake up.'

Irritably, reaching for the blankness of sleep, she shrugged off the hand and rolled over. 'Go 'way.'

'You're in my bed.'

Her eyes shot open, she became aware of her surroundings in an instant. The bed. In the cottage. And...István! Her head jerked around and they were eyeball to eyeball. 'What——?!'

'You fell asleep,' he said, his voice filled with affectionate laughter. 'I didn't have the heart to wake you. But you must get up and dress for the wedding——'

'Oh, good grief!' she exclaimed hysterically and pushed at his chest. To her alarm, he was in a bathrobe and exposing more of his body than she could cope with at that hour in the morning. Whatever that hour was. 'Stop leaning over me!' she husked. 'What time is it? Nine o'clock! Oh, glory, glory!'

Obligingly moving back, he watched her in amusement while she took stock, checking nervously that she still had her dress on beneath the duvet which decently reached to her chin. Then he leaned over her again.

'Your promise first, as a surety,' he said sternly. 'Promise you'll let the wedding go ahead with no revelations from you.'

'Well . . . you must realise my dilemma, István.'

'And you must realise that Lisa has to live her own life,' he murmured.

'But——'

His lips covered hers, softly, sweetly, and he was whispering flattery in between his kisses while her arms lifted to his neck and cradled his strong head. 'Do I have to keep you here after all?' he sighed. 'What would we do, while the wedding took place? How could we occupy ourselves?'

'Making jam!' she jerked out, wondering why she was kissing him back.

He chuckled. 'I thought it was always jam tomorrow! This looks remarkably like jam today.'

His hands reached beneath her, lifting her body to his and it went with alarming willingness. With light, sweeping movements, his fingers massaged her spine, moving downwards, ever down . . .

'István,' she said thickly. 'No.'

'You could hold me here, a prisoner,' he whispered, his tongue flicking around the curve of her swollen mouth. 'Both of us prisoners, perhaps.'

Helplessly she groaned because that would give her so much pleasure. And as his fingers continued to play with her bones, her flesh, awakening her whole body to his touch, she could feel all her muscles relaxing till she lay passive and ready to surrender.

'I want to go!' she said harshly, angry with herself.

'I don't believe you,' he said quietly. 'Haven't you realised yet that I'm not interested in Lisa, that I've been pursuing you all this time?'

She tried to think but he was kissing her neck, her shoulders, the line of her collarbone passionately and when he lifted his head and looked at her she saw that dark hunger in his eyes that made her tremble.

'I don't...!' She stopped in the midst of her sullen protest, stunned by the agony in his face.

'I want you,' he breathed fervently. 'Not as a light, passing interest, but as something more. The passion is there, I know it.' His breath rasped harshly in her ear, on her astonished face, his heart pounding in his chest with a frightening intensity. 'That's what Lisa has longed for, what she aches to know,' he whispered, firmly grasping her shoulders and taking possession of her mouth.

Tanya shuddered, moaning and whimpering, longing to respond with her own fierce kisses. And that was frightening. 'But if——' She tore her mouth away and pushed at his shoulders. 'If Lisa longs for you——' she began huskily.

'No, my darling!' he said softly. 'What I meant was that she longs to know a passion *like* mine. She knows what I feel for you. A helpless, remorseless, wonderful feeling that tears at my guts and makes me irrational, ruthless, and,' he smiled tenderly, 'so damn determined to make love to you that I'll do anything.' Tanya blinked, bewildered by what he was saying. 'And she's been worried sick because she hasn't felt the same kind of desire for John.'

'Which she feels for you...' Her croak was ended by István's kiss. The slide of his tongue, curling around hers, the pressure of his body unbearably, gloriously, insistent. And when he drew away, she wanted to pull him back because her own passion was beyond her control.

'Tanya,' he muttered gently. 'Don't you understand yet? She does love John, but in a different way. Neither of them feels the driving hunger that I do. They have a gentle, warm love. I reminded her that we're all different, that we all love in a different way, feel passion and desire at different levels of intensity. I persuaded her that she couldn't, shouldn't judge her love for John by my ardour for *you*.'

It wasn't true, she told herself, protecting her easily-wounded heart. But... 'You're telling me that you don't love Lisa?' she whispered.

'I don't love her. I don't want her,' he said simply.

'Oh,' she said inadequately. It was all she could manage. Something was beginning to explode inside her; a glimmer of hope, joy... He wanted her. She could almost believe him... But if there was no love, was it enough?

Slowly he eased himself off the bed. 'You're hard to convince! Perhaps we'd better go to that wedding,' he said in a strained voice.

'The wedding!' she wailed, wanting to stay and ask questions, to find out if he was serious. Had she misjudged him? Please, she begged the Fates. Let him not love Lisa! Please let it all be a misunderstanding on my part and not a trick!

He laughed ruefully and ruffled his hair. 'Don't look so edible,' he sighed. 'I can't bear it. That's why I didn't tell you my feelings last night. I knew I'd never hold back.' Dazed, Tanya swung her legs to the floor and held on to the side of the bed, trying to bring herself back to practicalities. 'Stay there looking half-ravished, and you can forget being a bridesmaid and spend the day in my arms instead,' he growled.

'Oh, glory, I'm a bridesmaid!' she gasped. 'I've got to get to the hotel and dress!'

'Don't panic,' he said gently. 'When I realised you weren't going to rise with the lark, I telephoned for someone to bring your clothes here. You'll be in time to help Lisa get ready.'

'But——' she said, bewildered. 'But——'

'There's a hot tub in the room beyond the bake-oven. Have a soak and I'll get you something to eat. You can't go without food till the reception at three o'clock and I refuse to let you go till you do eat. There is time. Don't worry.'

Confused, she allowed herself to be hustled to where a steaming tub sat in the middle of a flag floor. She blinked to see her dress hanging up from a picture hook. 'My make-up, the head-dress——' she wailed.

'All there, I think,' he soothed. 'The hotel housekeeper did her best. If anything's missing or wrong then you'll have to make adjustments when you reach the castle. Your dress is gorgeous,' he added huskily. 'I can't wait to see you in it.'

There was her dress, a honey gold, simply styled but beautifully cut and flowing softly to the ground as befitted a bridesmaid. A garland of coffee-coloured orchids for her hair. Her make-up box. The fine silk briefs she'd chosen so carefully so that they didn't spoil the slim-fitting, hip-hugging lines of the dress. *They*, she noticed, were warming with an enormous blue bath towel on a miniature stove! She blushed scarlet.

'The housekeeper who brought these here must know I stayed the night!' she gasped.

'Nothing wrong with that. We have a clear conscience, unfortunately! She imagines we were chatting till the early hours and lost track of the time. Don't forget,' he said, wryly, 'the world knows us as brother and sister.'

'Oh, yes,' she breathed in relief.

István grinned. 'Did I do wrong?'

'No, but—oh, get out and let me wash!' she said in agitation.

Action first. She had to get ready. Thinking could come later. Briskly she soaped herself in the deep, fragrant water and jumped out, wrapping herself in the cosy towel. In a few minutes she'd dressed, applied eye make-up and lipstick and whisked her hair up on top of her head. But she needed someone to help her with the orchid coronet. It would have to wait till she got to the castle, she decided and began to dwell on his extraordinarily quick summing up of the situation and his ability to organise everything in no time at all. He ought to be managing Oxfam, she mused, or some large disaster response team.

'Are you ready?' yelled István.

Hastily, she took a quick look at herself in the cheval mirror and picked up her skirts to dash into the main room. Where she stopped short. 'What's the matter?' she asked nervously, tugging at the straps of the scoop neckline. István's expression was so *odd*. 'Is it crumpled? Stained?' she groaned in alarm.

'No.' He cleared his throat and turned to lift some hot, freshly baked bread on to a wooden plate. 'You look fine. Come and eat.'

'Oh. Yes. I'm starving,' she said, disappointed that he hadn't been more flattering. She had been pleased with her reflection and had expected admiration at least. 'Fine' wasn't ecstatic enough. And then she smiled ruefully at her vanity and her eagerness to please him.

'You look posh,' she smiled. Understatement of the year! He looked devastatingly handsome in his morning suit. She arranged a huge linen napkin over her finery. 'You did sleep here, I suppose?' she added, peering over her enormous sugared doughnut.

'I was here, but I can't say I slept,' he said wryly. 'I've learnt to get by without sleep, though.'

'Is that a fact?' She digested that and a little more doughnut then slicked up the sugar with her forefinger. István's smudge-dark eyes were lingering on her lips and she touched them to see if she'd left any grains of sugar there. He leaned forwards and brushed her lips with his.

He pushed back his untouched plate and sipped the Turkish coffee. 'I expect people will think we've healed the rift between us, when we arrive together.' His eyes flicked up in appeal. 'We have, haven't we?'

'Yes,' she whispered, loving him so much that it was painful.

He reached out and grasped her hand tightly. 'Thank God!' he said shakily. 'Lisa will be so happy.' His chest heaved in a huge sigh and he rose from the table. 'Let me know when you're ready to leave,' he said shortly, and walked outside as though he couldn't bear being indoors any longer.

She smiled wistfully. István hated to be enclosed—in his private and emotional life as well as physically. That was why he'd never marry and why he never allowed himself to love anyone. He'd never stand the sense of being trapped. And that was why she'd be crazy to give in to his passion, or to her own. Passion waned. Only love survived. It would be wonderful for a while—and then what?

Except...if you never knew paradise, you never knew what you were missing. Wasn't that better than nothing, and worth the eventual disappointment? She wasn't sure. She really wasn't sure. And it wouldn't be long before István asked her to make a decision about their relationship.

CHAPTER SEVEN

PICKING up her handbag which the housekeeper had thoughtfully sent, Tanya went outside into the sunshine. Her tender gaze focused on István, looking like a bridegroom himself beside the brightly painted cart that had been prettily decorated with garlands—presumably for the wedding.

He helped her up to the buttoned leather seat and she carefully spread her skirts around her while he took up the reins and clicked the pony on. With a jingling of bells on the harness, the cart began to roll forward beneath the golden beech trees.

'Makes you glad to be alive,' he said quietly, stretching with pleasure.

Surreptitiously she eyed the expanse of glorious male chest and wrestled with that comment for a while. At the moment she seemed happy and sad and elated and depressed all at the same time. No wonder she felt confused!

They turned on to a wider track, protected from the searing Siberian winter winds and the fierce heat of summer by a long line of rustling poplars. And she thought with a sigh that she'd far rather have István and a little cottage—a simple life where they slept beneath big fat duvets and got water from a sweep-pole well and made jam—jam! she smiled wryly—than be rich and alone.

István was lifting a hand in greeting to a man in the village who was hugging and talking to one of his goats. A little further along, an old woman paused at the water pump and gave him a dignified nod. She saw his eyes linger on a group of children painstakingly painting the railings in front of their house and its pretty garden and she knew in her heart that he valued the simple things in life and loved him even more because of that.

He drew the cart to a standstill, waiting patiently for a herd of cattle to pass. They were in a sea of the long-horned cattle now, and she moved closer to him to keep her dress from their enquiring noses—and their horns.

'They've stopped,' she said, faintly agitated, and searched in her bag for her watch. 'We'll be stuck! What's the time?'

'We're OK, relax,' he soothed. The pony jerked forwards suddenly and Tanya's bag slipped from her knee. István bent to pick it up and slowly straightened. 'I think this is yours,' he said huskily. And handed over her open wallet, complete with its photograph of him.

She blushed. 'I kept it ... I put it there——'

'I see. Do you know what those photographs were in the cottage?' he asked softly.

'Family?' she hazarded.

His kiss landed on the side of her cheek. 'Some were. Most were pictures of you. I think,' he husked, 'there's time enough for a diversion.'

'Photos of me? Why would you—where are you going?' she cried nervously, when he began to turn the cart through the milling cattle.

'The church.'

Photos of her? She frowned. 'Will you stop being so unpredictable and unconventional and take me to the hotel!' she fumed. 'And answer a straight question and behave like a normal person for a change!' she wailed. 'Just this once——'

'I intend to.'

Photos of her. To hate? To remember, to... She bit her lower lip, dismissing any fantasy out of hand. But she couldn't prevent the small voice in the back of her mind that kept telling her why *she* had kept *his* photograph. Not to hate, whatever she'd told herself. It had been the only tangible evidence that he'd once smiled at

her, that there had been days when her heart sang with
joy because she was with her dear brother.

She tried, oh, so hard, to suppress hope and the
thoughts that winged through her active brain. Better
not to dream at all. Waking to the cold, lonely light of
dawn was so painful. She knew; she'd done just that.

But her heart refused to listen to caution and kept
trying to tell her to trust her instincts even while she dared
not admit what her inner voices were saying.

The cart was rumbling over cobblestones towards the
church. Tanya might have jumped out if it hadn't been
going so fast, if she hadn't been wearing such a special
dress, if... She smiled wryly. If she wasn't so fascinated
to know what he was up to.

Her eyes softened at the sight of the little church. It
had come straight from a medieval illustration with its
simple whitewashed walls and steep, wood-shingle roof.
Beside the church stood a separate bell-tower, tiled with
oak shingles almost to the ground and with a curious
balcony halfway up, its four corners decorated by small
turrets.

His muscular shoulders tense, his whole body
simmering it seemed with barely contained energy, István
jumped down and lifted her out eagerly, pulling her
almost unceremoniously into the little church. She had
brief seconds to register the astonishing red and green
painted interior and then he had taken her hands in his.

'Tanya, my dearest Tanya,' he said huskily, gazing
deeply into her eyes. 'Here in the church of the Huszárs—
oh, God!' he groaned. 'I can't believe this! With all my
heart and soul, I pledge myself to you.'

A rush of happiness threatened to swamp her. It was
true! Yet... she was scared. Frightened to believe him.
'Don't!' she said brokenly, shrinking back. 'I
can't——'

His hand held her averted chin fast, turning her head
relentlessly back to face him. 'You don't trust me, you
don't respect me,' he said quietly. 'And not till after the

wedding can I be totally honest with you. But you know
I wouldn't play false to you inside a church. This is my
family signet ring. If you do nothing else for the moment
take it,' he said, pressing it into her trembling hand, 'and
keep it till you know what happened in the past and you
understand.'

'István!' she said shakily, panic-stricken at her intense
desire to risk accepting his word. 'You were brought up
to deny your feelings! How can I believe——'

'Ester failed in that respect,' he growled. 'You saved
me, taught me love. Sisterly love to begin with. My own
mother has taught me the love of a mother for a son
and since I've been here I've learnt love for my fellow
man, admiration and respect for people from all walks
of life—people who've struggled and gone through hell
and triumphed against all the odds!' he cried passionately. 'Now you've taught me a different kind of love.
Tanya, I can love! It's been in my heart all this time.
I'm asking you to be patient till we can make our own
vows.'

'Our own vows! What are you saying?' she asked,
deeply moved. Her heart knew. It was soaring into space
somewhere. Only her innate sense of caution was holding
her back.

'Do you love me?' he asked quietly. His fingers
caressed her face with a sweet tenderness that drew a
soft moan from her lips. 'Do you love me?' And he
kissed her, reverently.

Confused, dizzy with love, she sighed and finally
surrendered to the inevitable. 'Yes!' she whispered, her
eyes luminous. 'Yes, I love you, I love you!' she sobbed.

'My darling Tanya,' he said passionately.

The kiss sent her to paradise. She wrapped her arms
around his neck and let her lips flower beneath his. I
love him, she thought. For good or ill, I can't help it.
The tragedy of his past had made him the man he was
and yet she loved him. Perhaps, she dreamed, tasting

the sweetness of his mouth, her love would make him happy.

'The wedding,' he breathed.

And then he'd grinned, caught her hand and hurried her out again, protesting, half-laughing, half-afraid and utterly bewildered. But so much in love that she felt like singing.

She was still shaking when she, Lisa and Lisa's personal music tutor processed from the castle to the church. The church where István had pledged to marry her. Or had he? She wasn't sure. Did an exchange of vows mean that? And she racked her brains, trying to remember if he'd said he loved her, then worried even more because she was sure he hadn't.

He'd kissed her when they'd emerged from the church, chivvied her along, talked about living together in some ranch where they could ride all day if they wanted, where she could operate her business. He'd suggested her father could live with them if he wanted to, or that he'd arrange whatever care necessary in England. But no mention of love.

She felt a chill deep within her bones. No mention of marriage. An arrangement had presumably been in his mind; a modern, sophisticated live-in arrangement, where neither of them had to make a final commitment, where István wouldn't feel trapped.

Tanya had fixed the ring securely in her bouquet. It had the same crest as the one on the bedhead in the little cottage. After the wedding she meant to ask him about the crest. The flowers shook from where her hands trembled so much and she gripped Lisa's train more firmly.

She had something else to occupy her mind.

There'd been a furore when she and István had turned up at the hotel together. Her sisters had been astounded, Lisa ecstatic, John speechless with fury. Whatever she said, he refused to hear, stubbornly yelling that István wasn't to be allowed near the church—and especially near Lisa.

It had taken all her persuasive gifts to get Lisa into her wedding-dress because the bride-to-be seemed worryingly reluctant. Even now, as they walked towards the church, Tanya wasn't sure that her friend would go through with the ceremony.

Suddenly Lisa stopped dead and turned around, her face white with strain. 'Tan!' she whispered. 'Do you *really* think John loves me?'

Tanya forced a smile, to calm Lisa's hysteria. 'Yes, I do,' she said gently. 'Or he wouldn't be so jealous of István. He's a bag of nerves,' she said reassuringly. 'Men! They're not really tough at all, are they?' she grinned.

'Oh, God!' groaned Lisa.

It had obviously been the wrong thing to say! Tanya feared her friend would turn tail and run at the slightest hitch. 'He'll forget his nerves when he sees you,' she soothed. 'You look absolutely lovely.'

'A princess bride,' said the tutor gallantly.

'He'll never accept the fact that István——' persisted Lisa.

'You know what he feels about him,' she reasoned gently. 'John has always felt inferior——'

'I *know*!' Lisa wailed. 'You don't understand——'

'You love him. You're marrying him. Forget István!' Tanya could hardly keep herself from yelling in her frustration and anger. 'We're almost at the church and it's beautiful!' she enthused. 'Even the wedding-car is out of this world!' With genuine admiration she eyed the white, open-top Aston Martin beside István's decorated cart.

But her fingers didn't relax their panic-stricken grip on Lisa's heavy brocade train. She might have to drag the bride into the church by it! she thought grimly, as they walked on. Villagers had gathered to smile and clap and call out their good wishes. When one of them smiled warmly at her, she vaguely registered that it was the woman who'd waved to István in the banqueting room and gave her a faltering smile in return.

'*Reggelt.*' Lisa's music tutor had paused to say good morning to someone.

'*Reggelt.*'

Tanya's mouth dropped open. István had taken the tutor's place and an adoring Lisa was gazing up at him as if the world shone out of his eyes!

'We're together,' he told Lisa, his voice husky as he returned the smile. 'It won't be long.'

'Oh, István!' Lisa sighed.

And Tanya felt the ice freeze her veins.

'Don't look like that,' István said, turning his head to her and grinning wickedly. 'Your turn next.'

The villagers crowded behind Tanya, chatting happily and pushing her on, a moving, frozen statue. Her turn. After Lisa? She gulped, telling herself she was being paranoic. But it was unlikely he was talking about marriage, so...

So they entered the tiny church, her heart thudding violently with alarm. John turned, his face appalled to see István in the role normally reserved for the bride's father, or for a trusted and highly respected man. She smiled brightly as though nothing was wrong; beaming at him and her sisters despite her stiff cheek muscles.

Every step seemed a nightmare. Music shivered in heart-wrenching sweetness into the air, a small choir of local people singing in the red- and-green-painted wooden balcony at the back of the church. István turned and smiled at her encouragingly but she ignored him, staring ahead as they moved up the aisle.

He wasn't going to play false, she told herself, bending like a stiff doll to arrange Lisa's train. He couldn't. He'd pledged himself to her in this very church.

Or... She licked her dry lips, her eyes hollow with worry. Had he done all that to ensure her silence...? Her breath rasped in and István flung her a worried glance. Worried for her, or worried for himself? He'd

told her that he'd keep her quiet about his visit to Lisa
one way or another. She knew how ruthless he was, tha
he'd stop at nothing to get what he wanted—and fo
reasons of his own, he'd wanted Lisa to be married.

Tanya's eyes closed tightly. He'd made her malleable
Moulded her, with empty promises. She fought t
prevent herself groaning out loud. If he'd been lying t
her and Lisa was pregnant, then——

Something pushed by her legs. Her eyes snapped open
to see a small child wriggling past, apparently eager t
see the bride. John bent down and picked up the child
his strained face softening. 'Later. *Késöbb*,' he said af
fectionately. He hugged the little boy and returned hin
to the embarrassed mother.

'Ohhhh!' wailed Lisa. With a rustle of her taffeta pet
ticoats she grabbed up her train and, to everyone's tota
astonishment, fled out of the church.

Followed a split-second later by... István!

There was a brief, hushed silence. Then Tanya race
down the aisle after them, collecting her wits faster than
anyone because perhaps she'd been expecting this al
along. Outside, she saw Lisa furiously revving up th
wedding-car and...

István leaping into it from several feet away.

'Stop, Lisa! Stop!' screamed Tanya. Helplessly sh
watched them driving off; the man she loved, eloping
with her dearest friend. 'You brute!' she whispered. 'You
planned this! You cruel, wicked, degenerate *villain*!
Heedless of her beautiful dress, she sank to the groune
and wept with anger and despair. The worst ha
happened. The very worst.

John ran to her side, grey with shock. Staggering t
her feet, she put her arms around him, hugging hin
tightly while the tears streamed down their faces. An
she made her own vow by that church. That István woule
pay dearly for what he'd done. If there was justice i

the world, one day she'd make sure he knew real pain, real despair.

She'd been warned about the Great Plain. The *puszta* was, apparently, the largest plain in Europe and she could well believe it. The road that had once carried cattle-drovers from Transylvania still shimmered with the same mirages that it had centuries ago. It was as straight as everyone had claimed—and as hot. It seemed to Tanya that a giant hand had been hard at work with a steam iron, pressing the awesome sheet of land flat so it could bake in the sun.

Even with all the windows open in John's car, and wearing the thinnest top and button-through skirt hitched to her thighs, she sweltered uncomfortably and was glad of the shady stretches of road between the tall poplars. Grateful too, for the long, cool drink she'd had at a wayside inn, a *csárda*, that had, appropriately, once catered for horsemen and outlaws. As a horseman and outlaw, she thought bitterly, István must feel comfortably at home here.

Checking the map, she found that she'd almost reached her destination: the address scrawled on an envelope addressed to István. Incoherent with fury, she'd felt no compunction in raiding his cottage to search for clues.

When she'd shown John the envelope, he'd turned away and refused to speak to her. He blamed her for what had happened, for not talking sense into Lisa. István had split her family again.

Leaving her sisters to cope with him, the guests and the return of the presents, she'd crushed the deep, dark well of despair inside her and substituted it for revenge. Taking John's car she decided to track the two lovers down. István had gone too far this time. He'd made a total fool of her and this time she wouldn't forgive him. Whatever he said, no matter how many lies he told her, she wouldn't be deceived again.

Flicking her glance to the driving mirror, she glimpsed two glittering and ferocious eyes. 'You don't know what's in store for you, István,' she murmured, grimly overtaking two Ladas and a Trabant all in one go, in a reckless burst of speed.

She too could fight fire with oxy-acetylene burners. He'd manipulated her by means of her sexuality. It would be a poetic justice if she could do that to him. István was a slave to passion and Tanya knew that if she really pulled out all the stops to be alluring, he'd find it hard to resist her.

It had first been her plan to trap him into proposing, perhaps even lead him up the aisle and then walk away, though she didn't imagine she would succeed now her initial wild rage had subsided a little—nor did she think for a moment she could do something so shameful.

Solemn-eyed now, she stared intently at the endless road. If she hadn't been doing this for people she loved, she'd be backing out and licking her own wounds somewhere in private. But she must *prove* to Lisa what a ratfink she'd chosen for a lover before she was hurt badly by him.

Her foot lifted on the accelerator. This must be it. Her throat dried up as she stopped to prepare herself. Beyond the fields of maize that stretched as far as the eye could see, sprawled a cluster of long, low buildings. The largest of these, sitting in a sea of poppies, looked like the *csárda*.

Quickly she slicked on some bright lipstick, unpinned her hair and undid two buttons on her skirt so that it would expose a goodly amount of thigh. It was hot enough, she decided, to wriggle down the stretchy straps of her T-shirt till they were off her shoulders.

A check in the mirror. Huge, excited eyes, 'loadsaflesh'. Oh, glory! Her pulses had reached take-off speed.

'I've got to be sultry,' she reminded herself. 'But not too obvious.'

The entrance gates further on announced that this was a riding school. And there was István, talking to a man by the Aston Martin. He was wearing tight black jeans and the traditional Hungarian shirt, open at the neck with romantic loose-flowing sleeves gathered at the shoulder. To her eyes, it seemed that he could have been one of the lawless horsemen from centuries ago. Despite his English upbringing, he was totally at ease in this environment.

She'd change all that!

Ice-cold inside, sweat damping her palms and body outside, she drove through a huge herd of snow-white geese and parked the car. She took her time getting out, giving him ample opportunity to study her legs where the skirt had fallen away with obliging ease. By the time he'd recovered his innate manners and had stretched out his hand to her, he was also staring down at her deep cleavage.

Coolly, she rose. 'You owe me an explanation,' she said levelly.

His smile of welcome vanished. 'You've saved me a journey. I was about to return and do just that,' he said warily.

'Of course you were,' she cooed, thinking *liar*!

Hand on hip, swing it out, sulky look of reproach. How stupid she felt! And some women did this as a matter of course!

He frowned. 'How did you find me?'

'There was an envelope in your cottage. I broke a window to get in.' Toss head as if in challenge. Lift ribcage. Breathe faster... She blinked. That seemed to be happening without any conscious effort.

'I rang but they said you'd gone.' István's frown deepened. 'No one would speak to me. I was worried——'

'Oh,' she said widening her eyes. Perhaps a little tremor in the voice wouldn't come amiss! 'Were you?'

Emboldened, he took her in his arms. She resisted just the right amount, she thought.

'There wasn't any time for explanations,' he said ruefully. 'I had to act quickly. Lisa ran off because John picked up that kiddie and he looked so darn tender and loving towards the child that she knew she couldn't go through with the wedding,' he said huskily. 'I didn't know what she was going to do—or where she thought she was going—but I jumped in the car after her and directed her here so I could help her work things out.'

Lift head and look admiring. Gaze into eyes in wonder. 'That was quick thinking,' she murmured. He gave a faint scowl. 'Well, where is she?' she asked breathlessly, going through the ritual she'd planned. Hair over one eye, looking up from under lashes. A little shudder, a wetting of the lips.

His eyes were narrowed against the sun. 'Hiding. Thinking, making decisions. You don't believe me, do you?'

Tanya knew she mustn't appear to be too forgiving or he'd be suspicious. 'I'm not sure.'

He looked at her thoughtfully so she fluttered her lashes a little and he must have been disarmed because he commented; 'You've done something different to your hair.'

'Oh, yes,' she said casually. 'I was hot. I let it down so the wind could blow through it.'

His arm stretched out as if unbidden and his fingers tentatively stroked her heavy swing of chestnut hair, his mouth becoming sultrier every second. Tanya seethed, loathing every inch of his hormone-driven body. He'd betray any woman for sex-on-the-spot! she thought furiously. But at least her task was going to be easier than she'd originally believed, and she hoped that Lisa was watching. And learning.

Deliberately she closed her eyes and assumed an expression of bliss. It wasn't that hard. His fingers had become emboldened at her lack of protest and had drifted to her neck.

'Please,' she husked in a helpless little voice. 'Don't. You know what your touch does to me,' managing to deny him and encourage him in one sentence.' And drew in a deep, breast-lifting breath. Was that right? she wondered, opening her eyes in a tempting little plea. Was it sexy? Apparently it was.

István looked drugged with desire. His expression drew a shudder of fiercely spearing pain from her that didn't need to be part of her act. He gave an answering growl in his throat and his mouth descended on hers before she knew he'd even moved.

Although she'd prepared herself for this moment, she hadn't expected him to respond so quickly and it was an effort to push herself into 'hate mode'. The protective mantra she'd composed in her head at the start of the journey was slow to surface and by that time István had already claimed total possession of her lips, her throat, her neck and smooth, satin shoulders.

I despise him. Barbarian, fiend, vampire! she began. 'Oh, István, don't!' she protested through pouting lips.

His hands were threading through her hair as he tilted her head up and kissed her with bone-melting tenderness. The warm sun blazed on her naked skin and warmed her as deeply as his kiss. For a crazy moment she registered the sensation of belonging in his arms, of freedom beneath the immense expanse of sky and the stark simplicity of the landscape.

Just in time she caught hold of her longing to stay here with István for ever. And strangled it. Hate. Contempt. Hate. Contempt. She'd known this wouldn't be easy. Thinking of John's anguish was enough to toughen her up.

'You're hot.' His finger brushed her forehead. Like two burning fires, his eyes smouldered into hers. 'Out here on the *puszta* you should wear your shirt loose, not tucked in.'

'I——' She lost the rest of her sentence somewhere.
The touch of his hands as he eased her shirt from the
waistband was a torment. Air flowed beneath, to the hot
slicked sweat beneath her heavy breasts and then...
'István!' she grated, making an involuntary movement
back at the slide of his fingers over her damp skin.

With a total disregard for her protest, he drew her
back again and pushed his hands back beneath her shirt,
gently stroking the swell of her breasts. 'Oh, forgive me!'
he muttered softly, as if realising what he was doing. To
her relief, his hands dropped loosely to his sides and he
looked at her helplessly. 'I hadn't meant to do that,' he
said, sounding surprised.

Amid her resentment of his appalling sexual hunger,
was a tinge of triumph. István could, apparently, lose
control. She was making progress.

She shrugged elegantly, ensuring that the strap slipped
further down her arm to expose the upper part of her
breast. 'We can't deny this extraordinary desire we have
for one another,' she murmured softly.

'No,' he muttered thickly, his eyes feasting on her
curves as though mesmerised by them.

Her teeth clenched but only the pressure of her nails
in her soft palms diverted her mind from the glorious
flowering of warm pleasure in her body. Hate. Hate. 'I
think I'd like to speak to Lisa,' she said casually.

'God, is she mixed up!' he grunted. 'She's wandering
about trying to sort herself out. I've no idea where.'

Pausing as though considering what action she should
take, she said tentatively, 'I want to hang around if that's
OK. I think I should leave her to make her decision alone
and not interfere. But she'll need me at some stage, I
think.'

He'd had time to make love to Lisa. But he wouldn't
do so again, she thought grimly. Not while there was
breath in her body!

'You always have to mother everyone, save them from
themselves!' he complained gently. 'Think of yourself

for once! God, when you offer devotion and loyalty to someone, it sure is forever, isn't it? You're swamping people, don't you realise? Give them space. Let them make their own mistakes, suffer their own hurt. What the hell do *you* want out of life, Tanya? When do you stop protecting everyone?'

Her slender fingers pushed back the hank of hair that had been flopping over her eye. It was annoying her. 'When they don't need me any more,' she answered huskily.

'And who judges that, Tanya?' he sighed. 'You?' He shook his head in mild exasperation. 'I think it's time you lived your own life and let the rest of the world make its own mistakes.'

This was her opportunity, she thought. Deliberately she lifted her foot and wriggled a finger around the instep, as though a small stone had lodged in her sandal. Her skirt fell open as she knew it would and István let out a long, slow breath. Then she gracefully put her foot down again and let the soft folds of her skirt swing back over the alarmingly bare expanse of brown flesh.

She let her eyes linger on his for a significant second or two. 'You know,' she said slowly, 'I'm beginning to think you're right. I have needs, urges.' Her indrawn breath lifted her breasts to him as though they were being offered. 'Out here I get the feeling that I want to run free, like those horses out there,' she said, gesturing elegantly to a dozen or so Lippizaner horses frolicking on the horizon. And to emphasise that fact, she raised her arms in a huge, sensuous stretch.

'Hell. Don't run too fast,' he husked. 'I want to be sure I can catch you.' And his finger insolently and accurately flicked her nipple, surprising her with the crude gesture that didn't equate with his usual seamless seduction.

Hastily she reclaimed the body she'd put on offer and bit back the scathing rebuke, substituting a rather watery smile. 'My knees seem to be rather weak,' she simpered. 'It shouldn't be too difficult.'

István looked faintly grim, but perhaps that was due to the effort of control. 'While we're waiting for Lisa to put in an appearance, shall we amuse ourselves?' he suggested in a strained voice. 'I could show you around.'

'Please,' she said demurely.

Putting his arm around her, he guided her towards the main building and István's hands were everywhere: stroking over her high buttocks, reaching beneath her T-shirt again and boldly caressing her breasts.

She thought a few small girly protests were in order and finally, when these seemed to have no effect other than to make him laugh and increase his caresses, she broke right away, trying to twist her clothes back into place.

'The Seven Veils are getting flung around a bit, aren't they?' he drawled. 'Not many more to go, by the looks of it. I do hope you're not expecting to get my head on a plate, like John the Baptist.'

Flushing, Tanya smoothed her top down and re-buttoned her skirt which his sneaky fingers seemed to have undone further than she'd wanted. 'You're rushing me,' she scolded with a flirty glance to keep him on the boil. 'My, it's so hot out here!'

'Steaming. Sorry, Salome,' he said casually. 'I was only responding. I thought you were hell-bent on seducing me.'

She stopped dead and flung him a suspicious glance but he was smiling engagingly. 'Slow down,' she murmured. His hand reached out and she moved forward again, alarmed by the urgent desire in his eyes. She must back-pedal! 'Tell me about your riding school,' she said slyly.

'Great, isn't it? It's not finished yet,' he answered with enthusiasm, and she breathed a sigh of relief that she'd hit on something that would divert his interest for a short time while she drew breath. 'It'll be mainly for tourists—

I suppose Germans more than anything, though I hope other Europeans will come too.'

'They'll stay in those lodges?' she asked, looking at the traditional-style steep-roofed houses scattered around.

'Self-catering,' he nodded. 'Those who want to learn to ride, to improve their skills or just hack out over the *puszta* can do so with expert tuition.' He took her elbow and turned her slightly. 'Further on, by the lake out there, there'll be a swimming-pool for the guests, boat trips, fishing, cart rides to see the racka sheep, shepherds, the ethnographical museum——'

Her heart thudded. It sounded like the place John's boss—the countess—had set up, the riding school whose franchise she badly needed. Anxiously her eyes searched his for clues, but found none. She had to probe further.

'John was talking about the woman who owns the Hotel Kastély Huszár,' she said, as casually as her agitation would allow her. 'She has a riding school too.' She gave a small laugh. 'Competition for you!'

'I don't think so,' he murmured, opening the door of the farmhouse and showing her into a large, airy hall. 'She's my mother. Both the hotel and the school belong to me.'

Her mouth gaped. 'But——! They belong to a countess! And John would never work for you!' she cried hoarsely.

'Of course he wouldn't! That's why my mother has dealt with him.'

'The countess?' She wondered if he was telling the truth. István was totally untrustworthy.

'That's right,' he said sauvely.

'I don't believe you!' she gasped.

'It's not obligatory.' His eyes were mocking. 'However, it was no coincidence that John landed that job. This way. We'll go outside, by the pool.'

Her mind whirling, she followed him through the hall over the cool tiled floor and out to the back of the house.

She'd banked everything on landing that contract. Now
István himself held the future of her business in his
hands! Her mouth firmed into a grim line. He wasn't
going to ruin that too!

She gazed vaguely at the lawn and flower-filled garden,
the artfully constructed private swimming pool that
blended with clever planting into the landscape and
reflected the glitter of the lake some distance away. The
crest, set into the terrace. She stiffened. It was the same
as the one on the napkins and the bedhead at Kastély
Huszár. This time, he was telling the truth.

'The cottage... It belongs to your mother,' she said
in a sudden flash of inspiration.

'Correct. Her housekeeper makes the jam,' he added
drily. 'A few of the staff at the hotel know me—and the
villagers of course, but generally I keep a low profile
and let Mother run the place. I visit her cottage, she
comes here. I think you've seen her once or twice.'

She frowned, about to contradict him, then; 'The
rather elegant, grey-haired woman?'

'Mmmm. She thought you were quite beautiful,' he
murmured.

'That's nice,' she said shakily. She'd liked the woman
immediately, one of those instinctive eye-contact re-
sponses. An overwhelming longing to have met his
mother and talked about the past, about István, was reluctantly crushed. They would never be friends. Not after
she'd finished with him. But...

She'd get the contract. By fair means or foul.
Struggling against the longing to give up and go home,
she made a big effort to look suitably worried about
losing the contract, but appealing at the same time. It
wasn't easy. How did women do it? Doe eyes. That was
it. Arranging herself seductively on a sun-lounger, she
looked up at István. Doe eyes blinked prettily at him.

'I was under the impression that the countess was going
to talk to me about sole British rights to the riding

school,' she pouted. 'You've really put the cat among the pigeons. Now what am I going to do?'

'That's an interesting question,' he said solemnly. 'I'm sure you'll think of something.'

Her eyes narrowed and she searched his face for suspicion finding none, however, to her relief. 'When John came to Hungary, hoping to court Lisa,' she said, 'he found it hard to find work and keep himself. It was very good of you to give him that job.' As she spoke, trying to flatter him and keep him sweet, it occurred to her that it was true. He'd been very generous, particularly as far as the salary was concerned.

'Can you understand why?' he murmured.

She wrinkled her brow. 'If he hadn't been manager of the hotel, with such good prospects, he'd never have dared propose to Lisa,' she said slowly.

'I suppose you're right,' agreed István earnestly, sitting on the edge of her lounger. 'I all but drove her into John's arms, didn't I? And gave them a promising future. How odd.'

Tanya frowned, not liking to think he was anyone's benefactor. 'But they didn't marry,' she pointed out. He'd made sure of that. Had he been offering with one hand and taking away with the other?

'That wasn't my fault,' he replied. 'I wanted them to marry.'

'So that she was available for you, but not hassling you to marry her?' she asked scathingly.

He winced. 'No. Because they love each other and I feel responsible for them.'

'After what you did four years ago, I should hope so!' The moment she'd said that, she regretted it. Keeping her temper with István was harder than she'd expected. Carefully she composed her face again. 'About the riding school. Would you consider——?'

István's fingers caught both of her straps and eased them down a little. 'There. You must keep moving these or you'll get strap marks.'

'Thanks,' she said faintly, finding his hovering face and the nearness of his body too much to handle for a moment. So she fixed her mind on landing the contract. 'I was wondering——'

'I'll order up some drinks,' he interrupted. 'Ferenc!' He rattled off a stream of Hungarian to a bright-eyed, beaming man, who seemed not in the least bit intimidated by István, but exchanged a joke or two with him before disappearing indoors again.

The sound of laughter and low, husky voices drifted out from the house. Tanya noted the gardeners, the men by the lake, others in the distance exercising horses and a group working in the training ring. She stood beneath an awning with a light breeze rustling the reeds in the trees and the lake beyond, the swallows flecking the sky with their darting acrobatics.

István seemed to have forgotten her and had bent to flip idly through the pages of a magazine on the table.

'Mind if I dabble my feet in the water?' she asked sweetly.

His cynical glance rested on her. 'Go ahead. Dabble.'

Knowing he was still watching, she swung her hips as she walked to the edge and hauled her skirt up before she sat down, hearing his hiss of breath with a malicious pleasure. The water was cool and silky on her hot legs.

'Your drink,' he murmured in her ear. '*Nektár*.'

'Thanks.' She took the fruit drink with faintly shaking fingers. 'István,' she said thoughtfully, 'this idea of yours about wanting European visitors to the riding school...'

'Mmm?' He was right behind her, not touching, but so close that she could feel the heat emanating from him. And his breath, fast and hard on her half-naked back.

She swallowed. 'I—I could be your English agent,' she said with bright enthusiasm. And turned slightly, with a little lean forwards, as well, to offer him some cleavage.

As she expected, his eyes didn't miss the opportunity she'd given them for a free ogle. 'What would I get out of that?' he growled huskily.

His mouth had curled into sensual lines and she knew she was halfway to success. So she leaned a little further, making him blink at the dangerous state of her top. 'We could negotiate terms. You see, I'm definitely taking your advice,' she said in as sexy a voice as she could muster. 'I'm thinking of my own needs.' Her inhalation of breath swelled her breasts in a spectacular style, and she almost took fright, becoming suddenly aware of the risk she was taking. 'I need—I need——' she faltered, swallowing at the intense look of hunger in the darkness of his eyes. 'I need——'

'I know what you need,' he said grimly and heaved her into the water.

He must have followed because their bodies met in an instinctive fusing of warm limbs, wrapping around each other. *Hold me*! she thought in desperation—not because she was afraid, but because that was what she wanted...

The feel of his flesh against hers. The hardness of his muscular frame. The strength of his arms enfolding her. The urgency of his male heat...

How could she!

Her head was wrenched back as they surfaced and the sunlight lit her face. István's mouth seared her lips with its branding-iron heat, his hands roaming everywhere, and then she felt the wet clinging of her clothes suddenly disappear and there was only one sensation: flesh on flesh.

'Uhhhh!' she gasped. Her eyes bolted open. She was virtually naked, his shirt had disappeared somewhere... 'István, please!' she mumbled, in between his passionate kisses.

Almost roughly, he pushed her to the steps of the pool and, quite heedless that anyone might see them, he lifted her in his arms and carried her to the grass, laying her down tenderly.

Her eyes closed languorously in the warmth, the sweet expectation too painfully exciting to bear. In glorious celebration of her womanhood, she stretched her body luxuriously, every taut muscle anticipating his touch.

'István,' she whispered dreamily. And lifted her body to his with the movement of a voluptuary.

CHAPTER EIGHT

THERE came the rasping sound of a zip, the rough dragging of material as István shed his wet jeans and briefs. She couldn't move or speak, the fear and anticipation paralysing her totally. Then he brought her to life again and she was gasping with the passion of his kisses, his caresses, his whispered words. Spasms of pain or pleasure—she wasn't sure which—tore at her breast as his lips teased and tormented and she slithered in glorious delight against his body.

'István...' She choked on his name, overcome by need as his limbs tangled with hers and his tongue bathed the throbbing peak of each breast in turn while his hands slid to the secrets of her inner thighs.

'I want you!' he muttered. 'You know I do.'

That evidence was hard and fierce against her, cruelly torturing her own emptiness, demanding an end to her terrible need. 'Please, oh, please!' she groaned in anguish. 'Make love to me, please, István, please!' And she writhed an abandoned invitation.

He gave a deep shudder. Then was still. His response never came. With an effort, she lifted her lashes. He was looking down on her impassively. 'I can stop if I have to,' he said hoarsely, the black glitter of his eyes quite frightening. 'I can control myself whenever necessary.'

'I don't—I—I don't know what you mean,' she gasped, panting with the violence of her feelings.

'Think about it!' he snarled and when she looked at him in bewilderment, he drew in his breath sharply as if it pained him. 'Which of us won that battle, do you think?' he muttered.

'Battle?' she croaked.

'In the fight between sex and the mind. Between the temptation of woman, the resistance of man. Eve, leading Adam into trouble, the usual kind of battle,' he snarled.

Tanya's eyes rounded at the hard, slicing contempt. 'You—knew what I was doing!' she whispered.

'Of course I knew!' he said angrily. 'I hoped you'd returned because you quite reasonably needed an explanation. So I began to coax you out of what I thought—at first—was your understandable state of wary hostility. Then I realised you were in earnest. I went along with your vamping to find out what you were doing and how far you'd go. All the way, it would seem,' he said through his teeth. 'Not only were you using your body for mercenary reasons, but you were looking for some kind of sexual revenge as well!'

'Yes! I hate you, I hate you!' she sobbed, sitting up.

He pushed her back to the ground and held her there, his eyes blazing. 'Tell,' he growled succinctly.

'Of course I wanted to get my revenge, for what you'd done to us all!' she yelled, wriggling beneath the pressure of his hands on her bare shoulders. 'I wanted to hurt you as you've hurt us! John's hurt, Lisa's hurt, I'm hurt——'

'I get the picture,' he said coldly. Putting his hands beneath her, he raised her up on her feet and pushed her roughly beneath a cold pool-shower, dousing them both with stinging cold needles of icy water that had her gasping. Then he turned the tap off.

'Stay there,' he hissed. 'I'll get you a towel.'

Tanya clasped her arms around her shivering body as well as she could and watched her clothes bobbing about on the surface of the pool. She'd failed, she thought glumly. In spectacular style.

'Here.'

Without looking at him, she wrapped the fluffy towel around herself and tried to hold it there. But her hands refused to function. 'Damn!' she muttered under her breath.

His face impassive, István tucked the edges of the towel tightly across her breast. 'Follow me.'

Shakily she stepped from the shower basin, and this time he made no attempt to be the gentleman and help her. She swayed, daunted by the tension in his body. And the fact that he was almost naked but for a small square of cloth hoisted around his lean hips. Miserably she averted her eyes and felt the blush of deep shame spread like a crimson stain over her sensitised skin.

'What are you going to do?' she whispered.

'This might come as a surprise,' he snapped, 'but I intend to talk to you. First.'

'F-f-first?' she squeaked.

'Yeah, first!' he growled.

He grabbed hold of her wrist and strode furiously indoors, taking no notice of her pleas, or the fact that they were dripping water everywhere, but hauling her unmercifully to a large bedroom with a beamed ceiling and satinwood floor. And there he flung her on the bed, his hand still encircling her wrist like a manacle.

He scowled at her as if he wanted to inflict pain and she trembled beneath the malevolence of his black, glittering eyes. 'You need taking apart and putting back together again!' he said savagely. 'You need your mind assembling in the right order!'

'Thanks!' she mumbled sarcastically.

Somewhere in the house a man began to play the violin, its haunting tone almost defeating Tanya and making her cry. But she choked the tears back and followed István with enormous, frightened eyes while he carefully, menacingly, locked the door.

The tone of the music deepened to a warm resonance that vibrated through her body. Then there was a rush of flirty swoops and falls, and finally hoarse, passionate notes, as though the violin was talking to her with the voice of a lover.

'Talk!' she croaked.

I loved you, she thought silently. I always loved you. And you let me down. The sound of joyous notes filled her head, the wild *csárdás* music that assaulted her senses and turned her brain to thoughts of pure, wanton abandon.

'I intend to,' he snarled, droplets of water flicking on her with the angry movement of his head. 'And you'll listen to every word. You'll hear my story and what I have to say.'

He glowered down at her and her heart gave a sickening lurch because he was more angry, more intensely bitter than she'd ever known. The water streamed down his cheeks on to hers, mingling with the tears that trickled from her huge, dismayed eyes.

'Stop that music!' she begged shakily.

'Why?' he scathed. 'Because it reaches your soul? Tugs at your heart? Are you sure you've got one?'

'Don't you know I have?' she whispered.

István's mouth tightened and he turned his back to her. 'That music,' he said harshly, 'is Croatian.' He collected a couple of towels and flung one at her, rubbing at his saturated hair with the other then pushing his hands impatiently through the tousled result.

Tanya silently dried her hair too, wondering what István wanted to say so badly that he was pacing up and down like a caged tiger. 'Who is playing?' she asked quietly.

'Ferenc. He's a refugee. So was my father.' His face was very still. 'My father was one of the most famous horsemen in Hungary.'

Tanya made some mutter of acknowledgement, not wanting to break his train of thought.

'Unfortunately,' he said tightly, 'there was a snag. Mother happened to be married to another man.'

'Oh!' Tanya bit her lip at the flicker of warning in his eyes and waited for him to go on.

He slung the towel around his neck and began to talk in a cold, detached way that made her shiver with apprehension. István hated her. He looked as if he'd set his mind on some unpleasant retaliation.

'Mother hadn't married for love,' he said unemotionally. 'But to preserve her home. Kastély Huszár had become State-owned and was falling about her ears. She vowed that she'd do anything to keep her heritage intact.'

'Even marry a man she didn't love?' frowned Tanya in disapproval.

'Why not, faced with that choice?' he growled. 'We care for our heritage, for our land, for the fact that we are Hungarian. Nothing and no one takes that from us, regardless of who is in power,' he said grimly.

'But that's inhuman!' she husked. And yet he thought it was admissible. It explained so much, she thought nervously.

'The Huszár dynasty goes back centuries. It's beyond personal needs. We have a loyalty and a duty to the family above that of our own,' István said in a cold manner that made her blood chill. 'Marrying an official from the Russian Politbureau and persuading him to run his office from the castle was worth the preservation of the estate for the future. Political regimes come and go. The land goes on forever!'

'You can't ever live purely by duty to your past; your mother discovered that in the end! Humanity stepped in,' Tanya reminded him angrily. 'She fell in love with someone else.'

'Madly, hopelessly.'

'How sad,' she said softly.

And to her surprise, there was an unhappiness in the darkness of his eyes that reached out to her with such intensity of feeling that she wanted to run to comfort him. But didn't dare. The rest of his tightly controlled body told her another story. If she made a sympathetic move, she knew that he'd reject her without a qualm because he regarded emotion as a weakness not to be borne.

'Love like that is dangerous,' he said harshly. 'It makes you act without thought, without sense. A madness comes over you when . . .' He frowned and controlled his voice again, which had become as fevered as his gestures. 'Well, Mother paid the price. She became pregnant during a time that her husband was on a long posting in Romania, overseeing the elections. She and Father had a desperate, yet blissfully happy affair.' His mouth twisted. 'Not that you'll know what I mean by that.'

'I do.' Her voice shook with emotion. She could feel his pain keenly because, unreasonably, it had the power to hurt her too. 'Presumably you were born before her husband returned,' she said huskily. 'Was that why you were taken over the border?'

'By Mother's maid—Ester,' he said gruffly.

'*My mother*! Of course!' Her body went stiff and alert against the pillows while István paced up and down, brooding on the past, driven by some urge to tell her the whole story. No wonder her mother had been half-deferential to István! 'This was when it was difficult to cross from East to West, of course,' she reflected.

'Illegal, without the right papers. Father died in an accident near the border, whilst trying to smuggle Ester and me and half the family jewels to the West. But he knew I'd got through.'

'Oh, that's tragic! I am sorry. You never knew him,' she sympathised huskily, her warm heart going out to István.

'I knew *of* him. Ester told me countless stories about a man who'd set Hungary alight with his daring and his expertise during those dark years of occupation,' he said softly. 'I admired him and tried to emulate him even when I didn't know he was my father. Ester was thrilled that I took after him in my love for horses.'

'He risked a lot for you,' she sighed.

'His life,' István said simply. He shot her a quick glance. 'Do you have my ring?'

She started. 'In my purse. I was going to return it to you——' To be exact, she'd intended to throw it at him, she thought miserably. With bitter words.

István's jaw tensed. 'Did you look at it? Did you see the family crest?' She nodded. 'And the flowers? The orchids around the band?'

'I didn't realise that's what they were,' she said slowly.

His head lifted and he stared out of the window at the distant line of the horizon. 'An orchid became the sign of freedom. We grew them in our hothouse at the castle. Father...' His voice grew low and husky. 'Mother told me that Father scattered them on the grass one particular night and made love to her by the light of the moon. That was her freedom,' he sighed. 'And how I was conceived, in love and joy. Later the orchid was adopted as the sign for the underground movement that helped people escape to the West.'

'That's terribly sad,' she whispered. 'And romantic.' Her thoughts were churning around, tenderness and sympathy mingled with her anger. Wryly she acknowledged that there was nothing unusual in that. István caused the most devastating havoc in her head.

'Ester doggedly used the money she'd smuggled over as she'd been told to: exclusively for me. It was her duty to see that I grew up worthy of my father—and capable of taking on the role she hoped I'd have one day in running the estates,' he said quietly. 'She became your father's housekeeper and when they fell in love they moved to Widecombe. In the previous village, there had been gossip that I was illegitimate and Ester not fit to be a vicar's wife. So in Widecombe they let everyone think I was their child. You know what village life is like.'

'But why didn't they tell you—and us—that you weren't our brother?' cried Tanya in exasperation.

He gave a short, mirthless laugh. 'They might have done. But, a little late, they realised that despite all their efforts to contain me I was hot-blooded and impetuous and alarmingly mature,' he said wryly. 'Apparently they decided not to risk their daughters' virginity by having me living in the house in the full knowledge that there was no blood-link between me and them. Keeping me in ignorance and banishing me to boarding school seemed the best bet.'

'Why didn't Mother send you back to Hungary?' asked Tanya earnestly.

'As I said before,' he replied gently, 'she knew she was dying and hung on to the last moment. I think she realised that I'd be furiously angry with her for not telling me before. I was hurt. I had a sense of betrayal because I'd had a right to know. The whole of my life had been a lie, Tanya!' he said fervently. 'I felt at that moment that I couldn't forgive her. And, as I said, I thought she was pretending she had cancer, to keep me in England.'

'She could have let you go and you could have come back——' began Tanya.

'I think,' he said more quietly, 'that she knew what would face me when I arrived at the castle and that I'd have no time for visiting. With nothing—as I thought—to draw me back to England, I became totally absorbed in the enormity of my task.'

'Restoring the house,' she said slowly. 'You were responsible for all the work at the hotel?'

He smiled and spread his hands. 'With these. Mother was living in penury, the castle in a terrible state of decay because her husband had been killed some years earlier in a street skirmish. Plunging in all my savings, I rolled up my sleeves and renovated the castle with some help, knowing that the fall of the Berlin wall would bring more visitors from the West and we could turn it into a hotel. DNA tests proved my ri_ht to the title and I bought back the land from the State.'

'It was an enormous responsibility,' she said quietly. 'I always thought you shunned that. I thought you cherished your freedom——'

'I had no freedom,' he said savagely. 'Never! Ester held me in a prison of her making. You held me in a prison.'

'I did?' she protested indignantly.

'Ester was always walking a tightrope with me and she knew it,' he said grimly. 'It was her duty to ensure I left

England. But she knew even before I did...' He turned abruptly to face Tanya, his face tense with pain. 'She had to clamp down on my sexual desires. But I don't have to do that any more. You yourself have released me from any hesitation I might have had.'

'You're not going to touch me!' she muttered, cringing back against the soft pillows.

He advanced menacingly. 'I am going to touch you *everywhere*,' he grated. 'In places you never even knew existed. We've always had a love-hate relationship. It seems you hate me enough to risk your own sexuality for the sake of revenge. So I'm turning the tables, Tanya. I'll make love to you and walk away without giving a damn.'

Her throat dried. Although she opened her mouth to yell, to protest, to beg, nothing happened. And he was covering her with his body, the muscles of his arms knotting beneath her marvelling hands, her body instantly melting towards him.

Your turn next, he'd said! First Lisa, then her! 'This isn't fair!' she breathed feebly into his damp, curling hair. Her mouth desperately longed to press against his flawless cheek, her hands trembled in the effort not to pull him harder against her straining body as he slid his hand beneath her back and raised her to him.

'*Fair*!' he raged. He thudded her fiercely back to the mattress, his eyes flashing with splintered light. 'If life were ever fair, I would have made love to you when Ester told me we weren't brother and sister! I realised I loved you——'

'You're lying!' she whispered hoarsely. 'You'd been in love with Lisa. She was losing your child——'

'I loved you,' said István with savage conviction. 'More than anyone, anything in the world. And when I knew I wasn't your brother, it was too late to tell you so because by then you despised me!'

A sob was wrenched from her body. Without knowing why, he'd felt the same inescapable pull of destiny that she had. And he'd channelled his feelings by seducing Lisa.

Against all her will, she felt her resistance flowing away with his hungry kiss, with the soft, adoring phrases and the torment of his touch. Lisa was in the past. It was over. Tenderly, almost reverently, his mouth travelled over her body, kissing with mounting passion every inch of her gleaming skin.

They folded to the ground together, and suddenly, that passion exploded into something wild and ferocious, so savage that it frightened her even while her frenzied little moans and pleas only served, she knew, to drive István deeper into its flickering flames.

Heat engulfed her, hotter than anything she'd known, hotter than her sensitised skin, his hot, heaving chest. They were both oblivious of everything but their mouths, their deafening hearts, their bodies, straining to ease their raging need for each other.

'I love you! I love you so much!' she breathed, her mouth delighting in the feel of the satin skin of his throat.

'Tanya!' he groaned. 'I love you!' he said savagely. His teeth roughly grazed along her shoulder and she welcomed the kick of discomfort because something had to distract her from the unbearable ache inside her.

'Touch me, *touch me*!' she begged in an anguished moan. Her voice sounded thick, weighed down like her body with a sensual languor. Flesh met flesh. Their bodies trembled and vibrated like violin strings. She felt her swollen nipples responding to the pleasurable pain of his fiercely arousing fingers. She was kissing him, raining kisses all over his face, then setting out boldly, uninhibitedly to suckle, bite and devour every inch of his body.

'Tanya,' he muttered thickly. His hands closed over her shoulders. 'I can't—I've got to—oh, God!' he groaned. 'I can hardly stop...'

'No, oh, please—please!' she cried arching her hips upwards in an unconscious demand. 'You don't need to... I want you. I love you——'

'Stop saying that...*please*!' he growled.

'No, no!' She ran her hands down his hips and he shuddered convulsively, his buttocks tense and hard beneath her fingers. She couldn't understand. He wanted her. She wanted him. The overwhelming waves swept over her conscious mind again, leaving only sensation. His harsh, urgent breath in her ear. The weight of his body. The glorious freedom as she prepared to give herself to him. 'I can't stand it any longer! Now, István! Now!'

For a brief, shattering second, she felt the hard maleness of him scald and quiver against her liquid softness. Tanya gave a low, primitive gasp at the depth of pleasure that gave her. Then, with a vicious oath under his breath, István, his warmth, his touch, had gone.

She lay there, shaking, moaning. Her eyes refused to open. She heard the unmistakable sounds of a man dressing. She squeezed her eyes tightly in pain, trying to forget the empty burning inside her and the fact that he'd brought her to the edge of sanity and abandoned her. Again.

'Why?' she said miserably. 'How can you be so petty——?'

'Petty?' he growled. 'No! Whereas you loved me so little that you could hurt me without turning a hair, I can't do the same to you—much as I relished the thought.'

There was the sound of a key in the lock as though he were leaving and she bolted open her eyes, cringing at the shuddering fury that trembled through every inch of his body.

'Don't go!' she whispered.

'I must. I can't take you,' he grated, 'because I love you too much. So you have your revenge after all, don't you? If you want it. Think that over.'

The door slammed in an explosion of sound before she could gather her wits together. She lay there, blinking stupidly.

He said he'd loved her. That he loved her now.

He'd given her a precious family ring.

He no longer wanted to hurt her—he claimed that he *couldn't bear* to hurt her!

Lisa was in the past, she knew that for a certainty. Whatever his mistake then, it was irrelevant now. Any tenderness he felt now towards Lisa had been the concern of a decent man for a woman in trouble.

He loved her.

'István!' she yelled, leaping off the bed. She was naked! With a groan, she ran to the big wardrobe and dragged one of his big loose shirts from a hanger, wriggling into it as she dashed to the door. Sobbing, yelling his name, she wrenched it open and stumbled outside. 'István! Where are you?!'

Frantically doing up buttons as she went, she ran through the house, startling the staff with her yells. And then as she paused for breath, she heard above her laboured breathing the sound of hoofbeats, drumming hard and fast on the ground. When she ran out, all she could see was a cloud of dust.

A man was watching her silently. A dark-eyed man with a violin in his hands. Ferenc? she wondered. 'Please,' she begged urgently. 'Where will he have gone? I must know! Tell me!'

Ferenc frowned and shook his head. 'No.'

'You can't be so cruel!' she wailed helplessly sinking to the ground.

She cried. There in the dust, she laid her head and let the tears soak a muddy pool around her cheek. People lifted her, muttering in Hungarian, and she felt the softness of a bed beneath her listless body.

He'd come back, she told herself. He'd come back before dark. And suddenly she thought of Lisa, leapt up and searched every inch of the ranch for her to demand an explanation till a young woman took pity on her and said that Lisa had gone.

All the fight went out of her. She sank into a chair till exhaustion caught up with her and she drifted in and out of a drugged sleep. Waking weak with despair, the paleness of her skin emphasised by the dark circles beneath her swollen eyes, she dragged herself into the shower and freshened up. Then, slipping into one of István's scarlet shirts, she went to the kitchen where Ferenc presided over the staff at the head of a long table.

'He's not back?' she asked huskily.

They all exchanged glances and said nothing.

'I love him!' she said in broken tones. 'I love him and he's hurting. Oh, Ferenc, if you feel anything for him at all, you can't let him love me and think I despise him!'

'I, *feel* for him?' The man let out a long breath. 'I would defend him against anyone—the Devil himself. Do you know what he's done for all of us here, what he does for others?' he demanded.

'He—runs a riding school and a hotel,' she began wearily.

'No, no, these are spare-time things,' he dismissed. 'The countess oversees the hotel. István's main occupation is to organise safe havens for refugees and find them jobs. He works for the cause of others who are rootless, who have lost their homes and sometimes their families. You see,' he said sternly, 'he understands this situation. And feels compassion.'

The room whirled. She sat down heavily. Yes, she thought, struggling to comprehend. *Yes. Of course.* He'd said he needed strength and stamina. He cared for the homeless. People without roots. Forced to abandon their families. His father had been a refugee . . .

'Oh, István!' she groaned and turned a look of utter hopelessness on Ferenc.

He studied her for several agonising seconds and then, 'Perhaps . . . Yes. I will show you where he might be. Come to his study.'

'Oh, thank you!' she croaked in heartfelt relief.

She followed the grave-faced man to a book-lined room and there, behind a paper-strewn desk, Ferenc paused and pointed to a huge map of Hungary on the wall. 'Here,' he said, his finger stabbing at a junction of path and river. 'This is where sometimes he goes to think and be alone, when he's exhausted from work, from the heart pain of others who lose their homeland.'

Tanya choked back a sob. 'Thank you! Let me borrow a horse,' she whispered gratefully. She would tell István she loved him and ask for his forgiveness. Her stomach felt hollow. She'd risk his rejection. Her eyes squeezed tightly together as she steeled herself to accept this possibility. Paradise or hell, she thought wryly. What a ride this would be!

In borrowed jeans and the scarlet shirt, she set off into the Hortobágy *puszta*, the great expanse of National Wild Park beyond his ranch, the garden and the lake. With hope and fear competing in a perpetual battle for her head and her heart, she kicked her horse into a gallop and thundered across the endless ochre plain towards the magical sea that shivered on the horizon; a mirage, of course, but magical nevertheless.

And the joy she felt when she saw his unmistakable figure by the river was almost unbearable.

'István!' she yelled. 'István!' She almost fell from her horse and straight into his arms, sobbing, incoherent. 'I love you!' she shouted. 'I'm not saying it because I want revenge or to trick you! I love you, you... you idiot, you fool, you——'

'*What*?' he roared, and held her at arm's length. 'Say it again!'

Apprehensively she studied his face. It told her nothing at all. She lifted her chin and met his eyes boldly. 'Again and again and again,' she said simply. 'I love you. Now what are you going to do about that?'

A grin split his face. 'Crush the life from you, if I don't ride some energy off!' He broke away from her

nd ran to leap up on his horse. 'Ride, Tan!' he yelled.
Come on! Ride with me!'

Without knowing why, or what she was doing, she
vas running to her horse too and in seconds was driving
ier heels hard into its glossy flanks, intent only on
:atching István.

He slowed a little, so they were galloping close together
hrough the dry taupe-coloured grass and wild purple
tatice. In the great grass plain beyond she could see
iorses running free, watched by mounted herdsmen and
:currying bundles of white woolly dogs.

The wind whipped her hair, stung her face. She loved
t. Every moment.

'Whoopeee!' she yelled.

Beside her, bent low over the black embroidered
iaddle, István laughed in sheer delight and urged his
snorting and high-spirited horse on, exhilaration in every
ine of his face and body. They rode till she ached, eating
ip the miles, scattering herds of geese and racka sheep
vith twisted horns, through the marshes with their whis-
•ering reeds and flocks of migrating birds that rode in
;reat clouds into the sky.

By a vast river, they slowed, panting too much to
peak, turning the horses and walking them sedately for
iome distance to cool them down. There was nothing in
iight, other than the river, the dazzling yellow of sun-
flowers beyond and the stark outlines of sweep-pole
vells, black against the searing blue-painted sky.

Tanya looked at István, her heart full of emotion. This
vas Hungary and she loved it. She shared a blood link
vith him after all, the same tendency to feel great passion
ind great love.

'Oh, István,' she choked. For a moment, there was
•nly the intense sound of buzzing insects as she tried to
'oice her feelings. 'I've found my paradise.' Tears began
o stream down her face. 'Why am I crying!' she wailed.
I'm so-o-o ha-a-appy!'

Chuckling affectionately, István vaulted from the saddle and drew her down into his arms. 'Oh, my darling,' he murmured tenderly. 'My darling, darling Tanya.'

Her arms lifted around his neck. She raised her face to his, her lips to his and in that simple gesture she mentally gave herself, body and soul to him, clutching at his damp hair and driving his mouth harder against hers because she wanted only to surround herself with pleasure. This wonderful, immense land, the sun's warmth, the bird-song... István.

'Come and sit by the Tisza,' he said gently easing back from her demanding mouth. From his saddle bag, he took a leather water-bottle. Beside the wide river, they sipped the water in contentment.

Tanya gazed out to the infinite horizon, imagining the nomadic horsemen of the past, galloping over the plain in a rumble of hooves and jingling harness. 'I'm so happy,' she said tremulously. 'Even happier than the old days before——'

'Before I vented my feelings on the world in general,' he said quietly. 'And you and I began to quarrel. I think it was because I cared so much about you,' he breathed. 'It worried me that I wanted to be with you and found you infinitely more interesting than other women.'

'Mother must have been worried too,' said Tanya soberly. 'If you'd known we weren't related, we might have become more than friends and that might have caused complications.'

'I couldn't understand why I cared for my sister so much,' he said ruefully. 'So I was deliberately foul to you. And hated myself for hurting you.'

She burst into a storm of weeping. It was too much to bear. He'd cared for her and had wanted to protect her. István was shattering every barrier she'd erected against him. Almost every barrier. There remained the shadow of his treatment of Lisa.

He let her cry on, holding her securely, murmuring nothing words in her ear. She thought of the days when he'd run to rescue her from danger, to protect her from rain or snow when they were caught out on the moors. He had the capacity to care, to love, to keep silent about the truth if it would hurt other people, and her heart swelled with love and admiration for him.

'I love you,' he whispered in her ear. 'I love you, Tanya.'

'You really do?' she asked hopefully.

'I do.' His hands cupped her tear-stained face and lifted to his. 'Oh, my darling!' he whispered.

'I don't really have a lover back home,' she said in a small voice. 'I—I haven't ever... *been* with a man,' she admitted timorously.

'Well you're pretty good at acting the siren,' he smiled.

They clung together and he rocked her in his arms. 'I want to tell Father,' she said softly.

'I'm telling the world,' he grinned, kissing her nose. 'Don't worry about your father,' he murmured, seeing her faint frown. 'He loves you and wants you to be happy. And I think he'll be relieved that, although he tore up my letters and prevented me from seeing you all to explain why I'd left, it hasn't mattered in the end. I'll make sure he's part of our family and that he's cared for. He gave me a home. He took Ester and me in and did his best to love me. It can't have been easy, with your mother stubbornly sticking to her promise that the money would be spent on me and no one else.'

His dark head was outlined by the great scarlet sweep of the sunset and she felt a lump of emotion collect in her throat. She'd never love him as much as she did now.

'You forgive him. You forgive us all. And you chose not to hurt me,' she said in a low voice. 'You could have made love to me and didn't.'

He looked down on her with such adoration that her heart briefly stopped beating. 'I've learnt control the

hard way. From birth I was taught to conceal m
emotions, to harness my passion. What does that te
you?' he asked gently. 'Don't you notice something od
about that? Isn't there something you think I've don
that doesn't fit with my rigid control?'

Her body trembled. With her huge, luminous eye
fixed on his, she knew that she wanted him; everything
Whether it was a good thing or not, he'd changed he
beyond all recognition. For love of István she was willin
to abandon all self-protection. Including the shiel
around her heart and the one that preserved her fron
the pain of knowing he'd...

She blinked, her brain connecting at last. 'Lisa...'

'Think it through,' he said softly.

Tanya passed a distracted hand through her hair. 'Sh
spent a lot of time with you, I suppose one day yo
found temptation too much to bear.'

'No. Try again.'

'You'd listened to her violin playing, talked to he
about technique and played some of your records t
her——'

'To encourage her. John was jealous because he an
Lisa were...' He stopped and lowered his eyes.

'Lovers!' said Tanya slowly. 'John and Lisa!' A col
sensation went down the length of her spine. 'She said..
Oh, dear heaven! She said, "It's your brother's..." Th
baby was my brother's! John's! It was his baby!' He
guilt-ridden eyes flipped up to his. Lisa had given he
the clue not long ago by saying that István had don
something totally unselfish! 'You took the rap! Why?'

'You'd jumped to the conclusion that it was me. I
seemed better you shouldn't lose your faith in John
You'd always defended him, loved him, protected him
Your reaction was so dramatic that I knew it would hur
you to know that he'd put Lisa in that situation. Yo
said that you could never respect a man who though
only of himself,' he reminded her gently.

'My reaction was extreme because I idolised you,' she whispered.

He winced. 'What a mess!' he groaned. 'I wanted your love and your admiration, but it seemed to me that I ought to sacrifice my own needs for the relationship between you and John. After all, I knew there would be repercussions that could destroy John's chances of eventually marrying Lisa. He was far too young to support a wife at that time, of course. Since I was already the "bad boy" in everyone's eyes, it made no difference to me what Lisa's parents thought. Better they should revile me than condemn John, who would one day, God willing, be their son-in-law.'

'You did that, for John?' she whispered. 'You even protected him from knowing his own mistake?'

'He felt inferior to me,' István pointed out. 'His self-esteem was low. Lisa knew that, and loving him, she begged me not to tell John that she'd lost his baby. How could I refuse?' he said, taking Tanya's hand in his. 'She was distraught. I only had seconds in which to sort out the situation so only one person was hurt. Unfortunately it didn't work out that way,' he added ruefully. 'But I couldn't reveal what had happened. For one thing, if John had known that I'd protected him, he'd have an even greater inferiority complex because I'd covered up his mistake.'

'Oh!' she groaned. 'No wonder Lisa admired you—no wonder she said you were misunderstood and she was in your debt!' A huge sigh lifted her shoulders.

'I was going to tell you after her wedding,' he said gently. 'Lisa and I didn't want to spoil it for you—and I thought you might not be able to hide your shock from John.'

'Lisa knew, didn't she? That you weren't my brother.'

'I told her when I knew you were coming to Hungary for the wedding,' he said gently. 'Four years had gone in a flash. I'd re-established myself, I'd done my best to forget you but without success. The thought of seeing you again...I felt...' He laughed wryly. 'I felt crazy with excitement. I knew I had to try and win you over but I was worried I'd blurt everything out and send you running back home! I swore Lisa to secrecy. She was so excited, because she thought we'd finally get together.' He grinned ruefully. 'It was so frustrating! I longed to rush everything but I knew you'd never believe me if I simply told you the whole, incredible story so I relied on your insatiable curiosity to keep you interested. My intention was to gradually lift a few veils, ring a few bells in your mind, till you began to think of me differently. I think I should have abducted you and kept you a prisoner till you finally surrendered your heart!' he chuckled.

'I'm far too stubborn! I would have never given in,' she giggled. Then her eyes clouded over. 'What are we going to do about Lisa's wedding?' she asked in dismay.

'Nothing,' István said firmly. 'Oh, she was upset when John picked up that kiddie. She was afraid to tell him about losing their child because she wasn't sure how he'd react. I told her to tell him everything, stick by him till he was convinced she did love him and always had, and to prepare for a double wedding.'

'A—double—wedding?' Tanya's eyes rounded.

'I pledged myself to you in the church,' he said huskily, kissing her fingers. 'And later I remember turning to you and saying it was your turn after Lisa. But I think,' he said, grinning crazily at her, 'we ought to insist on taking priority. I've got a den of wild things in my heart and my body. My needs are rather urgent, you see,' he husked.

'And mine...'

The last was muffled as they clung in a deep embrace. Joy filled her heart. He loved her. She loved him with every ounce of her being. They were to be married.

Looking dazed, he gazed down on her. 'We must ride back before it's dark.'

Contentedly, she agreed. They held hands as they rode, sometimes smiling idiotically at each other, sometimes pausing to watch chevron skeins of honking geese wend their way home, silhouetted black against the great disc of the setting sun. And when they returned, it was to find John and Lisa, sitting hand in hand outside in the darkness, wrapped in one another's arms as though nothing would ever part them.

Nervously Tanya watched István walk forward, saw John's start of recognition and then the two men were embracing one another fondly while she and Lisa cried in relief.

That night the four of them sat talking, explaining, laughing and hugging, till dawn. And Tanya rested her head on István's shoulder, proud of the man she was to marry and glowing with happiness. She was with the man she loved and that was enough.

Enough? It was *everything*!

* * * * *

If you enjoyed this book, watch out next month for UNCHAINED DESTINIES *by Sara Wood, in which we meet Tanya's sister Mariann—and her handsome Hungarian hero Vigadó!*

HARLEQUIN  PRESENTS®

Don't be late for the wedding!

Be sure to make a date in your diary for the happy event—
The eighth in our tantalizing new selection of stories...

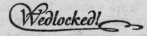

Bonded in matrimony, torn by desire...

Coming next month:

THE VALENTINE CHILD by Jacqueline Baird
Harlequin Presents #1795

Bestselling author of *Nothing Changes Love*

Valentine was the son Justin Gifford didn't know he had.
Zoe, Justin's wife, was determined to keep Justin out of her
baby's life.... Then Valentine needed help and Zoe knew
she'd do anything for him...anything at all....even if it meant
she'd have to *seduce* her *own husband!*

Available in February wherever Harlequin books are sold.

UNLOCK THE DOOR TO GREAT ROMANCE AT BRIDE'S BAY RESORT

Join Harlequin's new across-the-lines series, set in an exclusive hotel on an island off the coast of South Carolina.

Seven of your favorite authors will bring you exciting stories about fascinating heroes and heroines discovering love at Bride's Bay Resort.

Look for these fabulous stories coming to a store near you beginning in January 1996.

Harlequin American Romance #613 in January
Matchmaking Baby by Cathy Gillen Thacker

Harlequin Presents #1794 in February
Indiscretions by Robyn Donald

Harlequin Intrigue #362 in March
Love and Lies by Dawn Stewardson

Harlequin Romance #3404 in April
Make Believe Engagement by Day Leclaire

Harlequin Temptation #588 in May
Stranger in the Night by Roseanne Williams

Harlequin Superromance #695 in June
Married to a Stranger by Connie Bennett

Harlequin Historicals #324 in July
Dulcie's Gift by Ruth Langan

Visit Bride's Bay Resort each month wherever
Harlequin books are sold.

HARLEQUIN ◆ PRESENTS®

Harlequin brings you the best books, by the best authors!

MIRANDA LEE

"...another scandalously sensual winner"
—*Romantic Times*

&

LYNNE GRAHAM

"(Her) strong-willed, hard-loving characters are the sensual
stuff dreams are made of"—*Romantic Times*

Look out next month for:

MISTRESS OF DECEPTION by Miranda Lee
Harlequin Presents #1791

CRIME OF PASSION by Lynne Graham
Harlequin Presents #1792

Harlequin Presents—the best has just gotten better!
Available in February wherever Harlequin books are sold.

A family feud...
A dangerous deception...
A secret love...

by Sara Wood

An exciting new trilogy from a
well-loved author...featuring romance,
revenge and secrets from the past.

Join Mariann, Suzanne and Tanya—three very special
women—as they search for their destiny. But their
journeys to love have very different results, as each
encounters the irresistible man of her dreams.

Coming next month:

Book 2—*UNCHAINED DESTINIES*
Harlequin Presents #1796

Harlequin Presents—you'll want to know what happens next!

Available in February wherever Harlequin books are sold.

This February, watch how
three tough guys handle the

Lieutenant Jake Cameron, Detective Cole Bennett and
Agent Seth Norris fight crime and put their lives on the
line every day. Now they're changing diapers, talking
baby talk and wheeling strollers.

Nobody told them there'd be days like this....

Three complete novels by some of your favorite
authors—in one special collection!

TIGERS BY NIGHT by Sandra Canfield
SOMEONE'S BABY by Sandra Kitt
COME HOME TO ME by Marisa Carroll

Available wherever Harlequin and Silhouette books are sold.